GW00393904

FROM THE FOREST THEY CAME AND OTHER SHORT STORIES

New folk and fairy tales

Ant Marks

To David, fabio and the wonderful Diana.

Love and hugs

Ant MARKS

Copyright © 2021 Anthony Marks

All rights reserved

The characters and events portrayed in this book are fictitious.

No part of this book may be reproduced, or stored in a retrieval system,
or transmitted in any form or by any means, electronic, mechanical,
photocopying, recording, or otherwise, without express written permission
of the author.

antmarks66@gmail.com

Cover design and illustrations by: Trisha Kelland

This book is dedicated to my wonderful Grumplings

INTRODUCTION

Now, there is a man whose name is Ant. He loves reading folk and fairy tales and the telling of stories.

When his own children were young, he would make up tales that were totally farcical about what they were about to eat at mealtimes. On reflection it may have scarred them for life, but he thought his children found it interesting if not amusing.

Ant also loved to make up tales about who he was and where he originated from.

He once told someone he was the fifteenth generation of magical folk and he was the only male in the line since 1642. As very little history was recorded on common folk before then, Ant told tales of how the lineage probably went a lot further back than that. Ant has always had a very vivid imagination. It is not known just how many people believe Ant's tales about himself, but they do look at him a bit funny now!

Ant has so many story ideas floating around in his head, but had never put them down on paper before. Ant now has a new generation that he calls the Grumpling's and he is their Grumps, this name is of course ironic! He felt Granddad sounded far too old, especially as Ant still thinks he is seventeen and will often say, "I can still do all the things that I did when I was seventeen, they just hurt more and for longer."

With the arrival of the Grumpling's came a change, Ant started to write the stories down. He started to write new folk and fairy tales and didn't want unpleasant characters like many traditional folk tales had, that wanted to cause nothing but harm, he wanted a more feel-good factor to his stories so that all could enjoy, from the young to the old and everybody in between.

Ant started writing one after another. He was not intending to make a book at first from the stories, he just needed to get them down on paper, but once he started it became quite addictive. More and more stories kept coming, the stories were making sense of the world according to Ant, understanding and explaining just why some things are the way they are.

It was quite funny at first when someone said something and Ant would say, "Wait, I will just write that down, there's a story in that," but it must have been annoying when again and again he said, "Stop!" and nipped off to find pen and paper to get yet another idea down.

Ant has a beautiful wife called Trisha who he loves. He needs her to correct his grammar and punctuation, as he is not so great at that, in fact he thinks he is quite bad. Trisha is also a fabulous artist. Ant asked his wife if she could illustrate the book, thankfully Trisha agreed. Day after day Trisha went through the stories making the necessary changes, and spending hours drawing the illustrations.

Ant wrote stories about how the mistletoe got up into the trees, how the hare doesn't live in a burrow like the rabbit, why we no longer interact with the fairy folk like we did long ago and other observations on life that have happened to, or influenced Ant, so he took them and forged the ideas into stories that Ant hoped others might enjoy reading or telling.

So, if you ever should meet Ant be warned, you may just end up in one of his stories! Stuck between the pages for eternity. "Stop."

shouted Ant, he has gone again to grab paper and pen. For he thinks there might be a story in that.

Ant Marks 2021

FROM THE FOREST
THEY CAME

It was a cold morning and the first frost of autumn lay crisply on the ground. Joe and May had just got up and were putting on their warm clothes to go out into the nearby forest to gather wood for their fire. There was plenty in store, that they had collected over the summer months, but they always liked to collect more so it would dry and be ready for the end of winter as they didn't want to run out! The husband and wife did this every once in a while, just for their own peace of mind.

They took their hand cart and set off towards the forest, walking across the open grazed fields. The fields were beautiful in the summer, scattered with wild flowers, but now frost covered and a few wisps of mist were hanging low in the crisp air.

Joe and May stood for a moment and gazed across to the forest taking in this different kind of beauty, so white and crisp. May was looking into the darkest patch of the forest. "Look," she cried suddenly, "something is moving, there in the forest."
May pointed, with her arm and finger outstretched. Joe looked, and they both stood completely still, staring into the forest. Little figures started to appear from the darkness, May started to count them.

"One, two, three, four, five. Five!" she said in surprise. As the five little figures crept out of the shadow of the forest and into the field, Joe and May could see them more clearly. May said softly to Joe,

"They are children and not very old!"

Joe and May approached them ever so slowly and May called softly, "Hello." The children did not reply. They stared at Joe and May, then looked all about them and then back into the forest.

The children were dirty and cold and looked like they had not eaten for days, perhaps even a week. Joe took off his coat and gently tried to wrap it around all the children. They looked very wary and not at all happy about being wrapped by Joe's coat, but

soon found comfort in the warmth. May said,
"Are you with anyone? Where are your Mother and Father?"
Again, there was no reply from the children. Joe went to the forest
to have a look and shouted out to see if there was anyone with the
children, but there was no reply, save only for the birds. He went
deeper into the forest, still nothing, so Joe came back to May and
the children.

Joe lifted them up onto the little hand cart. There were three girls
and two boys all looking to be aged five or six. Joe thought to himself that they couldn't all be siblings, as they looked the same age?
Joe tucked his coat around the children as best as he could and
they all set off back home. As they travelled, Joe whispered to May,
"Where did those children come from?" and May replied,
"I wonder?"

Joe pulled the cart up to the door of their cottage and lifted the
children out. As they lifted them, Joe counted them out loud, as he
could not think of anything else to say, "One, two, three, four, five."
May opened the door and invited the children in, saying
"Come in, it's lovely and warm inside."

At first the children did not want to go in so Joe said softly to them,
"Don't worry, it will be fine. It's safe and warm in there."
Slowly the children entered the cottage, as they did so, they looked
all about them and as they went, they had a wariness about them.
May said,
"Joe, will you put some water on? I think I need to give these little
poppets a bath, then I'll find something for them to eat, they look
half starved!"
May got a saucepan and made some porridge sweetened with
honey, then into five bowls it went. May gave each child a spoon.
The children looked at the spoons as if they had never held one before, so May showed them how to use them and slowly they gained
the courage to eat the porridge.
Joe set about trying to find some clean clothes that might fit the
children. He went to an old trunk where they had kept some of

their own children's old clothes.

Joe and May's children had grown up, married and left home to start their own lives. May had kept their clothes in the hope of Grandchildren someday.

Joe also went to the neighbours to see if they too had any small clothes and explained about finding the children.

In the days that followed, the neighbours brought food, clothes and toys around, sometimes just as an excuse to see the children for themselves. The children were often asked,

"Where are you from?" but not a word came from the children. In fact the children had not spoken at all, apart from the tiniest of sounds to each other.

Joe and May sent messages out to all the surrounding villages to see if the children's parents could be found. No word came back, so messages were sent out further and further, but still nothing.

Several weeks went by and the children were now looking well. Neighbours were still sending gifts of food and clothing and Joe and May were most grateful for these things.

One of the neighbours had a cat that had kittens and when the kittens were old enough to leave their mother, the neighbour brought one around for the children. When the children saw the kitten they jumped up to have a closer look at it. The neighbour handed them the kitten and smiles came like a wave over their faces, one after another. The children were so careful holding the kitten, passing it to each other, taking turns, back and forth it went. No grabbing or fighting,

"That was unusual for children," Joe thought.

Later that evening, the children had gone to bed, all sharing the same bed, for they would not be separated. Joe sat in his chair near the fire and May sat in her chair on the other side of the fire. Joe said, like he had always done ever since the children had arrived,

"Where did those children come from?" and May replied,

"I wonder?"

The news of the children had travelled far and wide. On the odd occasion someone would turn up, saying that they had lost a child and were there to claim it. Some couldn't remember if the child they were looking for was even a girl or boy!

To others who came looking, May would ask if their child had a birthmark. Where was it and was it in an unusual shape? They would have a guess.

"No, we don't have that child." May would say as none of the children had any birthmarks, but May and Joe never told that to anyone.

A year had passed and early one morning there was a knock on Joe and May's door. Joe went to see who it was and standing at the door was one of the neighbours sons, who had moved away, but had travelled back to see his parents. He said that he had taken a shortcut through the woods on his way home and had found a hut in the forest that had burnt to the ground.

"Do you think this has anything to do with the children you found?" enquired the neighbours son, "it's about three days from here on foot."

Joe thought, then said,

"I think we had better take a look!"

Joe borrowed a horse and rode with the neighbours son to the burned down hut. They looked around but found nothing that suggested that the children could have been there. All they could find was burnt wood remains and ash, where the fire had caught the nearby trees, but luckily had not spread any further.

The neighbours son rode on, back to where he now lived and Joe rode home.

Joe explained to May that he hadn't found anything there and didn't think it was wise to take the children there.

"If they had been there, there was nothing and no one there for them now, and it might be just too traumatic for them," he said and May agreed.

The years went by and the children grew, three beautiful girls and two handsome boys. They did talk eventually, but didn't remember where they had come from, only that it had been very dark.

The children were an absolute delight to have around. They made Joe and May so happy and would help in any way they could.
Was it because all that time ago, before Joe and May had found them, that they had been made so scared of something or some-one, that they were so good? Or was it just because of the love Joe and May had given them every day since they had found them?

Joe still sits in his chair by the fire and May in her chair on the other side of the fire. Every evening, Joe still says,
"Where did those children come from?" and May still replies,
"I wonder?"

A SAYING FOR EVERYTHING

Once there was a woman called Evie. She lived on a dairy farm with a herd of cows that her husband looked after. Evie kept chickens. Not just one breed though, there was every kind you could imagine, every colour, shape and size that I think that has ever walked this earth.

Evie would sell their eggs from the farm house and on a small wooden table by the door, would be old jam jars filled with beautiful little flower posies that would be sold for a few pennies.

Now the thing about Evie is that she had a saying for, well just about everything, especially the weather!

One day the postman rode down the lane into the farm and gave Evie an unexpected parcel.
"Thank you Mr. Postman, I knew something would be coming, because on Tuesday the hem of my dress was turned up. 'If the hem of your dress is turned up, never turn it down, as someone will bring a gift around' said Evie in her lovely sing song voice.
The postman bid Evie a good day and rode on, he was quite used to her funny little sayings.

Evie had just set the parcel down on the kitchen table, when a small spider ran across.

"If you wish to live and strive, let a spider run alive."

Evie opened the parcel, it was some honey beautifully wrapped with tissue paper and ribbons with a letter from a friend, saying that she would like to come visit her. She said to herself,
"Well I can't remember dropping a fork. 'Drop a knife and a gentleman is coming, drop a fork and a lady is coming, drop a spoon and it will lead to disappointment but if it's a teaspoon that you drop it will be a surprise.'"
Later that day in the evening, Evie was with her husband sitting by the fire talking about the day, when her husband said,
"The hills were a bit foggy today, I wonder if it will rain?"
Evie replied, in her lovely sing song voice,
"'If there is fog on the hill, it will bring water to the mill.' Go outside husband, look at the smoke from the chimney, 'If the smoke is going straight up high, the day to come it will be dry, but if the smoke is blowing down, the next day will be wet that comes around.'"
"I could do without rain tomorrow!" and he went outside to see which way the smoke was going, then said,
"Oh, bother it's blowing down."
"Then there will be rain tomorrow." replied Evie gently.
As sure as eggs are eggs, it was wet the next day. It had started to rain early in the morning.
Evie said,
"Don't worry husband, 'rain before seven, fine after eleven.'" and sure enough, the day cleared up before lunchtime and her husband could get on with his work.

A few days later Evie's friend came to visit her.
"Hello my dear, how wonderful it is to see you again. It's still a bit chilly, is it not spring yet?"
Evie welcomed in her guest then replied,
"Well, spring never starts until the last jasmine flower has fallen, or when you can stand on five daisies on the lawn, that is when spring is finally here."

The friend laughed and said,

"Well I do hope we have a lovely summer, what do you think Evie?"

"I think August should be good, 'a wet March is a fine August,' and 'if the ash comes into leaf before the oak, we are in for a soak,' but this year it was 'the oak before the ash so we will only get a splash', so I think this summer will be fine.'

Her friend was very used to Evie's sayings and smiled warmly.

As the two were chatting over a cup of tea, a magpie flew past. Evie quickly said,

"Good morning, good morning."

"What was that about?" asked her friend.

"Oh, it was only a magpie, I just had to say that before it flew out of sight or it's bad luck…'One for sorrow, two for joy, three for a girl, four for a boy, five for silver, six for gold and seven for a secret never to be told.'"

Later that day, Evie's friend left to go back home, very happy to have seen Evie but perhaps a little confused from all Evie's sayings!

May came and the weather had been lovely. As Evie looked across the meadow with its flowers all yellow, she thought,

"I wonder if they are buttercups or dandelions?"

She walked over to have a closer look and said to herself,

" When the meadow is full of yellow with the buttercups, the summer will be hot, but if the yellow is not, and dandelions are all you've got, the summer will not be better for it is likely to be wetter."

There was a footpath that ran through the meadow and Evie spotted a man strolling along the footpath to get to the village. All of a sudden there was a very loud humming sound coming from the sky, it was a swarm of bees. Evie and the man stood watching them as they flew overhead and then disappeared over the trees. Evie said,

"Now, that was a sight to be seen!"

"Yes indeed it was." replied the man, and then he said,

"A swarm of bees in May is worth a trailer full of hay, a swarm in June is worth a silver spoon, but a swarm in July ain't worth a butterfly!"

Evie's face lit up,

"You know that saying too!"

"Oh yes," said the man "and many more, they help us to remember things...How to tell the weather, when to sow seeds, bring in the harvest and to look after the world in which we live. We shouldn't squash a black beetle, for that will make it rain. One of my favorite sayings is for when it snows, 'old mother goose, pecking at her geese, selling the feathers, a penny a piece. I think it reminds us that one goose has two o's but more than one, you use two e's for geese.' Who knows where they came from, but I think it's a lot of fun."

"I love old sayings too" said Evie and bid a goodbye to the man and walked back home with a smile on her face. As she walked there was a gust of wind that lifted the leaves on the trees, and Evie said to herself,

"It's going to rain, for when the trees show their petticoats, the rain will come to push them down."

That evening it did rain, but just as Evie had predicted, that summer was warm and dry. So perhaps there is something in the sayings from long ago.

THE HARE

L ong ago in the distant mists of time, the hare like the rabbit, lived in a burrow, a hole dug in the ground.

One day, Hare thought to itself,

"I don't like living in a burrow as my home. What would happen if it caved in and I can't dig my way out? Or if it rains so hard that it floods my burrow, or a stone rolls and blocks me in, what would I do?"

Hare had always been a bit of a worrier, and it was so worried about all the things that may happen, that it could not sleep or even rest! Hare went out of its burrow and looked up to check the sky for rain.

Rabbit was also out of its burrow, but Rabbit was just happily nibbling grass. Rabbit looked at hare then looked up at the sky and said,

"What are you looking at Hare?"

"I'm checking the weather." said Hare, so Rabbit asked,

"But why are you checking the weather?"

"I'm checking that it's not going to rain." replied Hare.

"The sky is clear, it's not going to rain!"

"Well it might," said Hare, " I don't want it to flood my burrow and I don't want to be in there when it does!"

"Well mine never has and I'm sure yours never has, so why worry about something that's never going to happen? We always dig down and then up, so if water does run in, it can't reach where we are!" Rabbit was rather amused by Hare's worrying!

"But what happens if the burrow were to cave in, and I can't dig my way out? What then?"

"Well mine has never caved in and I'm sure yours hasn't either. Do we not pick places with roots that hold the burrows up to prevent just that? So why worry about something that is never going to happen?"

"But what if a stone was to roll over the entrance to the burrow and I can't get out? What then Rabbit? What then?"

Rabbit shook its head and said,

"Like you I have more than one way in, so there is more than one way out and it is very unlikely that if a stone should roll over the burrow, that another stone will roll over the other way out at the same time! So why worry about something that is not going to happen, I think sometimes you are quite mad Hare!"

Rabbit went back into its burrow and left Hare still gazing at the sky.

One evening later, the rabbit found hare still staring at the sky.

"Are you still checking to see if it's going to rain?"

"No," replied Hare, "I'm watching the moon!"

"Why are you watching the moon?" said Rabbit most bemused!

"I don't trust that moon," said Hare, "it might fall and squash me, so I'm keeping an eye on that moon."

Rabbit sighed and shook its head again,
"The moon is not going to fall, just like your burrow is not going to cave in or flood or be blocked in by a stone!"
"Oh, I don't live in that dirty old hole in the ground any more, that will cave in, or flood or a...." Rabbit interrupted Hare,
"Where do you live now then?"
"I live above ground now. My home is in the tall tufts of grass where they have bent over. It keeps me dry if it rains, most of the time, anyway I like the rain."

Rabbit turned away and said to its self,

"That Hare is quite mad, I'm telling you, Rabbit, Hare is mad!"

So if you should ever see a hare gazing up at the moon, it is just keeping an eye on that moon!

DANNY DAYDREAM

Danny was a daydreamer. When he was at school, he was always staring out of the window in a daydream.

"Stop daydreaming Danny," the teachers would say to him.

"I'm not daydreaming, I'm thinking." Danny would always reply.

Danny was a bright lad, but he was always off in a daydream.

When he was old enough, Danny went to work in the local stone quarry. The stone was split from the quarry face, then carefully cut into neat blocks with a hammer and chisel.

Danny's job was to move the blocks once they had been cut. He had to pick them up, put them on a small cart and push them quite some distance to the road. Then he would carefully lift them off the cart and stack the blocks, where much bigger horse drawn carts could collect them. It was a tough job and it took quite some time as the carts had to shunt back and forth to turn, so that they could take the stone off to the stonemasons to be used in buildings.

Danny had been doing this for some time, when of course his mind would start to wander and was not on his work at all. The quarry boss looked at Danny and saw that he had drifted off into his own world. The quarry boss shouted,

"Stop daydreaming Danny and get on with it!"

"I'm not daydreaming, I'm thinking."

The boss went quite red in the face and called out in a rage,
"You are not paid to think boy!"
"Well, perhaps you might want to pay me to think once I have told
you what I'm thinking!"
The boss was slightly bemused by Danny's cheeky reply and said,
"Well, out with it then?"
"I have been thinking. What if we extend the road, round here to
where the blocks are cut, then with a u-turn, take the road back to
join with the main road. When the big carts come in they wouldn't
have to shunt back and forth to turn, they could drive straight in,
then drive straight out again." Danny continued,
"then I wouldn't have to load them onto the cart, push it to the

road and stack them there. I could just stack them here, ready for the carts. It would be much quicker. "

The boss replied in amazement,

"Well in all my days, we have been doing it the same old way for as long as I can remember, and no one has ever thought of that before!"

A few days later the road was put in and just as he had said, it was much quicker and easier for Danny to stack the blocks.

One day, one of the big carts rolled away by itself. It went over a steep bank but luckily a tree stopped it from going too far and overturning, or worse still, from smashing up.

All the men from the quarry ran over to try and push the cart out. It was of no use, the cart was far too heavy.

Danny stood watching, his mind started to wander again. One of the quarrymen said, "It's no use daydreaming Danny, that won't get the cart out."

"I'm not daydreaming, I'm thinking." Danny replied. The quarryman jeered and said,

"Why, do you think that will help?" and laughed at Danny.

"Yes, I think that it will help."

"Oh right!" said the quarryman sarcastically and laughed at Danny again.

"Get me a long rope, a short piece of rope and a pulley wheel." instructed Danny.

Once Danny had all of these things, he pushed the short piece of rope though the centre of the pulley wheel. Then he tied the short piece of rope around a tree just past the top of the bank. Danny then took the long rope, tied it to the cart then pulled the rope around the pulley wheel and down the bank.

"Right, now get as many men as you can, get on the rope and pull down hill. Anyone else, get behind the cart and push it up." called Danny.

All the men either took to the rope or pushed the cart. Slowly, to the quarryman's amazement, the cart began to move up the bank and finally up to the top onto the flatter ground.

"How did you know that was going to work, Danny?" said the quarry boss.

"Well, I just thought about it! It is easier to pull down hill than it is to pull up, that's all!" Danny replied.

"Do you know something Danny? You really are something quite special!" said the boss.

Many days later, Danny was working, stacking the blocks, when his mind started to wander again as it had often done before. The quarry boss looked at Danny and saw that he was away in his own world once more, not stacking the blocks as he should have been doing. The boss shouted out,

"Are you thinking Danny?"

"No," Danny replied, "I'm daydreaming!"

"You're a cheeky lad Danny!" The quarry boss laughed!

I SEE THEM TOO

L ucy had just turned six. The summer days were long and warm and Lucy would spend most of her days playing in the garden. It was a large garden with woodland at the bottom of it, an orchard to one side and a kitchen garden on the other that went up to the cottage where she lived.

Lucy had a younger brother who was three, she was not interested in playing with him yet, there was something else that had captured her attention that long, warm summer.

Lucy would stand for hours just staring into the trees at the bottom of the garden.

Lucy's parents were worried about this, so one day they asked her, "What are you looking at?"

"I'm looking at the little things that fly between the trees." Lucy replied.

Her parents looked. They stood very still and stared into the trees focusing really hard and then they too could see flitting about.

They could see flies buzzing. They could see the odd butterfly that danced across the garden, sometimes two, turning and twisting around each other like two well rehearsed ballroom dancers. They also noticed a dragonfly and dandelion seeds that were being swept up and carried away on the warm summer breeze.

Lucy's mother said, "Is it the butterflies and the dragonflies or perhaps the dandelion seeds that you see?"

"No," replied Lucy, "they are like little people flying in and out of the trees and then they just disappear."

"What, a wonderful imagination you have." said Lucy's father.

"There's one!" Lucy said, pointing to a big oak that stood a little way back from the edge of the garden.

"Oh, now it's gone! Did you see it?"

"No," replied Lucy's mother, "but I have an idea."

Lucy's mother went into the cottage, then into a cupboard where there was an old box. The box contained some things that had belonged to Lucy's mother when she was a little girl.

From within the box she took out an old, dusty and tattered book of fairy tales.

Lucy's mother opened the book and showed Lucy, saying "Do they look like this?"

Lucy looked and flicked through the pages one after another.

"No, not really." she replied

Lucy's father said, "Do they have pointed ears, like that?" as he pointed at another page in the book.

"Well, I don't know, I have not seen their ears as they are covered by their long flowing hair, but they do have pointy noses." explained Lucy.

"What about their clothes, are they like these, all different colors?"
Lucy's mother asked as she looked through the book.

Lucy replied,"Oh no, they are all the same and I don't know if they
wear any clothes at all. I can't see any collars, cuffs or seams, but
they don't look naked."

"What about wings, do they have any?" Lucy's father asked in a
teasing way with disbelief.

"I can't see wings, but something is a bit blurry and almost misty
behind their backs."

Lucy's mother asked, "So what color are they then?"

"They're not blue or green or grey, more a sort of mix of all of
them, a bit like that stuff over there on that tree." Lucy said, whilst
pointing up at something growing on a tree branch hanging over

the garden.

"That is lichen." Lucy's father said.

Lucy said, "It's a bit like that color, but sometimes darker or greener or sometimes more blue."

Later on that same evening, Lucy was getting ready for bed. She looked out of her bedroom window, down across the garden and into the woodland. She could see a faint glow coming from the forest floor and around it, Lucy could see tiny little bright specks, darting back and forth as if dancing around it. Lucy wished she could have got closer to see more clearly.

But Lucy was tucked into bed.

Lucy's parents were down stairs. They started talking about what Lucy had said she had seen.

Lucy's father said, "Well that daughter of our's sure has got a vivid imagination!"

Lucy's mother agreed, but deep down, the descriptions that Lucy had given kindled a memory from a long time ago, since forgotten. A memory from when she was a little girl, in a different place.

The next morning there was a knock at the door. It was Lucy's grandmother, who was coming to stay for a while. Lucy loved it when her grandmother came to stay, she was warm, kind and would tell stories about the cottage and when she was a little girl. For in that very same cottage, Lucy's grandmother had grown up. Lucy ran up to her and gave her a big hug, then took the grandmother's hand and led her outside. They walked down the garden and then Lucy stopped, fixed to the spot and stared into the trees. Lucy's grandmother looked at Lucy and then into the trees.

She then turned back to Lucy and said, "You can see them too!"

"Can you see them?" asked Lucy.

"Yes," said the grandmother, "I always have!"

MAKING POTIONS

Elsie was a little girl who loved playing outside. At the house where she lived, the garden was full of beautiful flowers. Elsie would skip around picking the flowers that grew in the lawn, but she knew not to pick flowers from the ones that grew in the borders that lay by the edge of the lawn.

The flowers that Elsie picked were carefully placed in a basket, then taken to a low brick wall where Elsie would work from. There were lots of small bottles lined up on the wall, with cork stoppers on the top, Elsie was making potions! This was Elsie's most favourite thing to do in the beautiful garden.

Elsie picked up a small old bucket then skipped next door to the blacksmith, to ask if she could have some of the water that he had quenched the hot iron in, for this is the best water to make potions with.

Elsie asked the blacksmith,

"Please may I have some of that water?" and she pointed to a large half barrel full of water. The blacksmith replied,

"Of course you can Elsie. Are you making more potions?" The blacksmith was quite used to Elsie coming around for the water.

"Yes I am."

"So what potions are you going to make today?" he asked.

"I'm not sure. I'm going to ask people what they would like my potions to fix."

"Now, that's a good idea, very useful." said the blacksmith. Elsie

asked him what he would like a potion for. The blacksmith said,
"Well, my hands are so rough, dry and cracked, from working with
the iron, maybe a potion for that?"
Elsie replied,
"Now that would be useful." then skipped back home with her
bucket of water and put it on the wall next to the basket of flowers.
Elsie's grandfather came out to see what she was up to. The grand-
father said,
"Are you making more potions Elsie?"
"I am Grandfather and I need to know what potion you might
need, so that my potion can fix it."
The grandfather thought, then said,
"Well, how about more hair on my head?" and he picked up a
big piece of soft green moss, popped it on his head then danced
around, like only a grandfather could, saying,
"I will look so fine and dandy with more hair." It made Elsie laugh,
and she rolled around the grass with glee.
Elsie and her grandfather didn't notice, but sitting up in a pear
tree near them, with it's blossom so white, were two little fairy
folk watching their every move and listening to their every word.

Elsie started mixing the potions, one for the blacksmith to make
his hands soft and smooth, just as Elsie had promised. She took
some of the pink flowers, ground them up, then put them in one
of the little bottles and added some of the water from the little old
bucket. She then picked up the cork stopper, but just before she
put it on the top, one of the little fairy folk lent forward, waved its
hand and said some strange words and then sat back in the pear
tree and giggled.
Elsie picked up another little bottle, took some blue flowers from
the basket, ground them up, put them in the little bottle and
added some of the blacksmith's water from the little old bucket.
But again, before Elsie could put the cork stopper in, the other one
of the fairy folk lent forward, waved its hand and said some more
strange words then sat back in the branches of the pear tree and
they both sniggered cheekily.

Elsie's mother came out into the garden and called,
"Are you having fun out here?" The two fairy folk replied,
"Oh yes, we are!" but no one could hear them.
"Yes Mother. Can I make a potion to fix something for you?" called
Elsie back.
"Well yes, as it happens, I could do with an extra pair of hands to
help me with all the work in the house, like the cooking, washing
up, cleaning the clothes and house."
"Then I shall make you a potion that will give you an extra pair of
hands to help you with all of those things." Elsie replied
"Oh that will be nice." Elsie's mother said with a sigh.

Elsie reached over to the basket. She took some yellow and white
flowers, ground them up, took another little bottle, and put them
in, adding some of the water from the little old bucket. She mixed
it up, then popped in a single white flower that floated on the top
of the potion. Again, before Elsie could get the stopper in, one of
the little fairy folk lent forward and waved its hand saying more
strange words. Then sat back in the pear trees branches and giggled with the other one.
Elsie put the cork stopper in then said,
"There. Three potions."

She skipped to the blacksmith, gave him the little bottle and said,
"Here you are, one potion to make your hands nice again."
"Thank you Elsie, I will put it on now." he said gratefully.
Elsie skipped back home and gave the second potion to her grand-
father saying,
"Here you are, this will put hair back on your head."
"Oh, thank you Elsie I will put it on straight away." said the grand-
father, then rubbed it into his head.
Elsie finally went and found her mother and said,
"This one's for you, it will give you the extra pair of hands you
need!" Elsie gave her mother the third little bottle. Elsie's mother
said,
"Oh thank you Elsie, but where should I rub the potion on me?"

Elsie replied,

"On your hands, that's the place where it shall work best."

Elsies mother tipped the potion out onto her hands and it made them very wet. Then she put her hands on either side of Elsie's face and kissed her forehead.

The next morning the whole house was woken up by the grandfather making such a noise, shouting,

"Look, look! It's black and curly! My hair was never black nor was it curly, what has happened to me?"

Then there was a knock at the door. It was the blacksmith, he said,

"Look at my hands, they are like a lady's hands, all soft and smooth. What has that potion got in it?"

"Only flowers from the lawn and water from your barrel. Come in and have a cup of tea and take a look at grandfather's head." Elsie replied.

"I will fill the kettle, get the cups and put the tea in the pot." and with that, Elsie filled and warmed the kettle and made tea.

They had all sat down to have the tea, when Elsie said

"I will get us some biscuits from the jar." Once they had finished, she said,

"I will just wash the cups and put the tea things away."

"I think I have just found my extra pair of hands!" laughed Elsies mother.

After a few days the blacksmith's hands had turned back to how they were, perhaps just not so rough and cracked.

The grandfather's hair wasn't so black or curly and there was not so much of it.

Elsie's mother kept her extra pair of hands though, as Elsie helped wherever she could. Elsie still liked to make potions, but this time, people weren't quite so quick to try them out.

So if you ever make potions, make sure the little fairy folk can't hear you!

◆ ◆ ◆

RICH MAN, POOR MAN, NOT A BEGGAR MAN OR A THIEF

Once there was a rich man that worked hard at making money, for that was all he cared about. He helped no others and took them for all he could. He would tell himself that he was better than others, that he was cleverer than others and sometimes he would even tell them so too! He would say to himself,

"I want for nothing, for there is nothing I can't buy."

He had his big house, he had his servants that did everything for him, cook, clean, and wait on him for his every need.

The rich man had a poor neighbour that lived nearby. One day, he saw the poor man out tending to his garden.

The rich man called to the poor man,

"Hey poor man, I have everything and you, well you have nothing!"

The poor man called back,
"Why neighbour, that is not true. I believe that it is I that have everything and it is you that has nothing!"
"How so? called the rich man. The poor man replied,
"Well I have love and you have not. I have a wife and children and you have none!"
"I have servants that love me."
"Servants?" laughed the poor man, "Ha! If they were offered more money elsewhere, they would leave you, is that not the truth?"

The rich man was getting quite cross by now and called back,
"Well, I could take a wife if I wanted one."
"Yes you could no doubt, but would it really be you that she is in love with, or would it be the lifestyle and money that you can provide, that she would really be in love with? True love, affection and trust is earned. There is nothing more rewarding, more than any coin can bring. Children will come and that love is unconditional. I will do anything for my family and that is true love itself. You can't even get that from your dog, for a dog's love may seem un-

conditional, but that is only until someone else brings it a bigger piece of meat!"

The rich man thought for a while, then replied,

"At least I don't have to beg!"

The poor man called back,

"It is not I who has to beg. I always have enough to feed and give my family comfort, it is you that has done the begging!"

"When have I had to beg?" cried the rich man.

"Well, how many times have you had to plead for a customer to buy your trade or to seal a deal? Is that not begging?" said the poor man.

The rich man thought again, this time for even longer as he did not want to be out done by the poor man. He called back,

"Well, at least I have not had to steal!"

The poor man was very quick to reply,

"I have never stolen, it is you that's a thief!".

"How can I be a thief," shouted the rich man angrily,

"I have money."

"So, how many times have you, in your deals, offered so much, but then in truth delivered so little? How many times have you told your customers that this 'is the finest you can buy', when it is nothing but a cheap copy? Or indeed, how many times have you taken money and not delivered anything at all? Is that not a thief?"

The rich man thought again, and said gruffly,

"I am rich because I can buy grain and hold on to it until all other grain supplies have all but run out. Then I can lift the price and you have to buy it, your money will feed my pockets! This makes me very rich and very clever indeed!"

The poor man needed no time to reply to that,

"You starve the poor to line your pockets, holding back and then over charging them! You will never find true love like that! I will not pay high prices for food, for I have real knowledge. I will go and glean food from the hedgerows and the forest, rather than put

money in your pockets. Perhaps then, it is I who is clever?"
The rich man thought, and thought.....and decided not to speak to
the poor man again for he did not like the truth.

And the truth is that the poor man was not poor at all as his wealth
came from the love and warmth of his family. It came from the
land that provided his food. He was truly rich in life.

THE WASSAIL

The new year had not long turned and a cold deep frost had set in. In a small village there lived a young lad. His name was Rufus and he was so named due to the bright red mop of hair he was born with. He was also known as Rue by his friends.

Rue was looking forward to the celebrations of the wassail, to give thanks to the fruit trees and to drive out evil spirits in the hope of a good harvest in autumn. This happened each year in the orchard in the village.

This year was to be a very special wassail for Rue as he was now of the age where he could carry one of the fire torches in the procession, which led from the village green through to the orchard.
In the few days leading up to the wassail, the villagers were all a buzz about the preparations, dressing the fruit trees with brightly colored ribbons and little bells and building a bonfire with all the prunings from the fruit trees.

Rue had been thinking about what the old boy would say about trimming the trees. That was what the villagers called him, as he must be over a hundred years old. He would tell them,
"You've got to prune the trees into a goblet shape so there is nothing in the middle, always to an outward facing bud, so the shoot goes out not in and remember to cut out any wood that crosses over one another!"

Rue had one task, to make his fire torch. He needed a thick pole of new green wood so that it did not burn through too quickly and the fire lit end drop off. Next he had to bind it with layers of sacking, with each layer having a covering of tar. The torch had to last the whole of the procession but it didn't need so much tar that it would drip burning flames on him or anyone else.

Rue had not realised how stressful it was to get the fire torch right! Rue then twisted wire around the sacking so that when it was burning it wouldn't unravel. Once Rue had made the fire torch, he sighed in relief that it was done and could only hope that it would be alright.

Then he thought about all the singing and dancing that would take place at the celebration. Everyone dressed up in costumes made of small pieces of rags that flapped about when they danced, each with their faces painted in bright colours.

The day of the wassail had finally arrived, final preparations had been made and people were starting to gather on the village green for the fire torchlight procession that began just as the sun had set. The first torch was lit then the next, one torch to another, until all were ablaze. The procession set off, a fiddler started to play, then the drums and some people had long staffs with bottle tops all over them so they made a chincking sound as they hit the ground. Children ran in and out of the procession with pretend fire torches with red and yellow ribbons hanging from the top of a stick and everybody started to sing the songs of old. The whole road down to the orchard was lit up, it was a magnificent sight to be seen.

As the procession entered the orchard, one by one the people threw their fire torches onto the bonfire. The flames got higher and higher as more and more torches were thrown on and then finally, it was Rue's turn to throw his torch on. He had made it, his first fire torch procession!

By the fire was a large bowl filled with warm cider, beer and honey mixed with winter spices. The villagers were filling their mugs from it, still singing. There was such a buzz of happiness in the cold night air.

The Lord of the village stepped forward and took to a small stage that had been built, all went quiet. Rue stood in the silence as the lord asked the reverend to bless the fruit trees to bear fruit for another year, then a poem was read.

"On the trees on every bower,
Sets a bud that births a flower.
Then when springs warmth doth come,
Bring the honey bee with it's hum.
Swell the fruit with sun and rain,
So we can't have the green man's blame.
And when the fruit with ripeness, cheer,
To celebrate again the turn of year."

The Lord then took a tankard of cider and poured it on the roots of as many trees as he could, and urged all the villagers to spill a little of their drink on the roots of the fruit trees too. The Lord then shouted,

"Wassail, good health to all and may the trees fruit well."

The music started again and so did the dancing, it carried on all night until the early hours of the next day.

When Rue finally got back home, he laid in his bed, his mind still buzzing from the celebrations, thinking of the dancing, the fire torch procession and the few kisses that he had stolen from the girls that he had danced with!

"Oh what a marvellous night," Rue said sleepily to himself.

Each year the wassail took place, but each time the celebrations seemed to get less and less. It was now not as exciting as Rue had remembered on that first day when he had carried the fire torch. Then finally one year, the wassail didn't happen.

Spring came that year, the fruit trees didn't flower well at all and by the summer there was hardly any fruit to be seen on the trees.

The villagers called a meeting with the Lord. One of the villagers stood up and said,

"What are we going to do about the orchard, my Lord?" The lord replied,

"I think the orchard is old and useless now, it needs to be ripped out, and we can then grow something else."

Rue could not bear to think of the orchard going, it had stood proudly in the village since he could remember.

Rue stood, shaking, as he was not used to talking in a public meeting. He started speaking with a bit of a stutter which he never usually did,

"I, I think we need to bring back the wassail, if we do that the trees will fruit well again." A big cheer went up from the crowd.

The Lord spoke again,

"Well Rufus, you have until the end of next spring to do it, or the orchard will have to come out! You have a big task ahead of you, not just one fire torch, but the whole wassail to organize!"

The old year had passed and a new one had just begun. Rue had one task, one big task! He collected more ribbons and bells to tie in the fruit trees than ever before. He then organized a 'best costume' competition to get the villagers to dress up more than they ever had. All the young lads of the village set about making their 'first' torches with as much care as Rue had done when he was young. He also built a much bigger bonfire and organized it to be just as exciting as it had been all those years ago when he had first carried a fire torch.

The evening of the wassail came. The fire torch procession set off with a fiddler playing, then the drums, followed by villagers carrying the staffs with the bottle tops on. When Rue looked down the road to the orchard, it was just as magnificent as he had remembered it.

The flames from the bonfire leapt up so high, it must have scorched the heavens!

The Lord asked the reverend to bless the trees, the same poem was read, as it always had been since that first wassail and Rue carried

his own fire torch. The Lord poured cider on the roots of the fruit trees, then shouted,
"Wassail, good health to all and may the trees fruit well."

The Lord came over to Rue and said,
"Rufus you're a fool, but I love it!"
Music and dancing went on until the sun was just about to rise just as Rue had remembered when he was a young lad.
That spring the fruit trees flowered so well and in the autumn more fruit than ever before.
From that day on the wassail was never missed, and the orchard is still there to this day.

Next time you pass a fruit tree, just thank it and shout
"Wassail, good health to all and may the trees fruit well."

SHINING STAR

In a little village faraway, there lived a little girl and in the same village lived her Grandfather.

Every day just before bed time the Grandfather would visit. If when he visited and the sky was clear, he would take the little girl by the hand outside to stare at the stars.

They looked up and after gazing for a while, the little girl said, "What are the stars?"

"They are people that have gone from this earth to somewhere better and they are looking down on us so they can see that their families are all doing well." replied the Grandfather.

The two of them stood and looked and looked at the wonderful night sky.

"What is that Grandfather?" said the little girl pointing up at the night sky.

"Ahh, that is a shooting star. Quick, make a wish! That is a star that has fallen out of the sky," the Grandfather explained.

"Why has it fallen?" asked the little girl .

"Well, that is a star that has decided to return to earth to be reborn as somebody new." replied the Grandfather.

"Do you see that bright star up there?" asked the Grandfather.

"Yes," said the little girl.

"Well, that is your Grandmother looking down on you with a big smile and that is why she shines so bright, because she is so happy to see you." said the Grandfather.

"Will Grandmother fall back to earth and be reborn again?" The little girl said.

"Maybe one day, but for now she is patiently waiting to see you grow up." replied the Grandfather. "Also she is waiting patiently for me to join her up there."

Then he pointed up saying,

"Do you see those two stars right next to each other?"

"Yes," said the little girl.

"Well, they were two people so in love that they are still with each other up there in the sky and their twinkles even look like they are holding each other's hands. That will be what your Grandmother and I will be like when I get there." the Grandfather said.

"And me too Grandfather?" asked the little girl.

The Grandfather just smiled and said,

"We must go inside and warm you up before bed."

One day passed into the next, winter into spring, summer into autumn and then again into winter. The years passed and the grandfather still came each day to visit.

One dark chilly late autumn evening the grandfather had not come to visit. The little girl, who was not quite so little any more, said,

" where is Grandfather?"

The young girl and her parents went to see the Grandfather. He had been taken ill and had not been able to get up out of bed. The young girl's parents sent for the doctor, but the next day the Grandfather passed away. The whole family was very sad, but that evening the sky was very clear.

The young girl said, "Let us go outside." So they held each other's hands and went outside.

"Look up at the stars," she told her parents, "that bright star is Grandmother," and as they looked at the star, right next to it was the faint glow of a new star forming.

A PUPPET THEATRE

Albert loved to spend as much time as he could in his uncle's workshop. Albert's uncle was a cabinet maker and a very fine one too. He would put the finest details into his work, inlaying flowers and leaves cut from different coloured woods or carving swirls and twists into the wood.

People would come from miles away to commission Albert's uncle to make fine creations for their homes.

One day as they were both sitting in the workshop, Albert's uncle said to him,

"Well Albert, today we have a new commission from the manor house in the village."

"What is it?" asked Albert.

"They would like me to make a puppet theatre, of all the things!"

"A puppet theatre?" Albert looked surprised. He wasn't used to his uncle making anything like this! He had only ever seen him making wardrobes, dressers, dressing tables and other pieces of furniture.

"Have you ordered the wood yet?"

"This time," replied his uncle, "I'm going to use all the wood that I have left over from other jobs. It's about time I cleared out the wood store. You know what I'm like for saving offcuts of wood, waste not want not! Think of the profit I shall make on the piece, not having to buy any wood! I will need your help to make this, I need your small hands to put small pieces into their place."

Albert was very excited, he had always wanted to work with his uncle,

"Oh yes, I would love to help!"

On that first day the frame was built and put together. The next job was to cut out a large circular piece of wood that was to be made into part of the theatre floor. It was held with a spindle through the centre with small pegs that went all the way around the spindle.

Albert had to fix the small pegs into place, carefully glueing them into a hole that his uncle had made.

Albert then had to fit more small pegs into a smaller circle of wood. A long shaft was pushed through the side of the theatre, then attached to the smaller circle that butted up next to the larger circle's pegs.

"What is this for?" Albert asked.

"Just you wait and see." replied his uncle.

The uncle showed Albert how the pegs fitted into one another, then fixed a handle to the end that stuck out of the theatre side. When the handle was turned, the large circular piece of the theatre floor also turned.

"There you see how it turns? That is so the little puppets that are put on it, appear to be walking around the stage!"

Albert shrieked with excitement, he had never seen anything like that before,

"Wow that is wonderful!"

"Do you like that?" asked his uncle.

"Yes I do, it's amazing!" replied Albert.

"Now we need to make some puppet people. I'm going to draw them on wood and you can cut them out."

Albert's uncle drew lots of people on to some wood and gave Albert a saw with a very thin blade.

"That's a fret saw, isn't it." The uncle nodded and asked Albert to clamp the figure onto the bench,

"So half of it hangs over. Then cut around the line, but not my bench! I'm going to find some fabric to make the curtain for the theatre."

Albert started to cut but found that he could not keep to the lines and then he snapped off one of the legs while trying to cut out the other.

Albert's uncle came back with the fabric and Albert turned to his uncle with a tear rolling down his cheek,

"I can't do it, I'm no good, I have failed."

"Do you not want to do it any more?" Albert's uncle asked him gently.

"I do still want to, yes." said Albert.

"Then you have not failed, if you get it wrong and try again, then that is the only way to learn. Someone who says they have never failed has probably never achieved anything!"

"Here, I will show you and we will do it together."

Albert and his uncle cut out all the figures. There was a king, a wood cutter, a fairy, a wizard and many others.

"There, we did it together, my little workmate." said the uncle once they had finished all the figures.

"Yes we did, we really did." Albert was so very proud of what they had done together.

"It's going to be a woodland theatre," explained his uncle, so the two of them cut out trees for either side. They then cut out more tree shapes for inside the theatre and made curtains that could open and close with a pull of a cord.

Albert's uncle painted all the people with such fine detail, some were on sticks and some had slots that fitted into the turning floor of the theatre.

Albert helped paint the rest of the theatre and he took his time and painted very carefully.

When everything was finished the uncle asked Albert,

"Well what do you think? Do you like what we have done?"

"Oh yes, I love it! They are so lucky at the manor house. Can I come with you to deliver it?"

"Of course you can." replied his uncle.

The next day Albert and his uncle put the theatre onto a cart, then set off to deliver it.

They went past the church, the carter's pond and then Albert's house.

Albert's uncle said,

"Shall we stop to say hello to your mother and show her what you have helped me with?"

"Oh yes," said Albert, he couldn't wait to show off all his hard work to his mother.

The cart stopped outside the house, Albert jumped off and ran inside.

Albert's uncle lifted the theatre off the cart and followed him into the house.

"We were just coming out to see it," Albert called to his uncle, "you could have left it on the cart."

Then Albert's uncle smiled and said,

"It was never really meant for the manor house, this is yours, for all the help you have given me."

Albert's face lit up with such a smile and he could only just get out the words,

"Thank you" as he hugged his uncle.

SOMETHING FOR
YOUR JOURNEY

Violet loved to walk for days and days along all the main well trodden tracks, from village to village and town to town. Now this was a long time ago when travel was only by horse or on foot. Violet lived in a thatched cottage with a rather unusual garden. There weren't many flowers or a grassy lawn, it was all turned over to grow fruit trees of all kinds. She also grew nuts, wild garlic, raspberries, wild strawberries and many other edible plants. She would grow them, not just for herself but also to be planted elsewhere.

The long warm days of summer had passed, autumn brought the wonderful vibrant colours to the trees and the soil was damp once more.

Violet had started to lift all the plants and trees that were ready to be replanted elsewhere, gently wrapping their roots one by one in damp paper and then tying them carefully. Violet would then pack the plants and trees into her bag, it was quite a large bag, for a new journey was about to begin.

Each year, Violet would plant trees and plants, all the way along the old well travelled tracks. This she had done for almost as long as she could remember. She planted wherever she was able, within a weeks walking distance from her home.

On this particular journey, Violet had decided to go further than she had ever been before. To get a good head start, Violet was going to take a stagecoach and with everything packed that she would need, tomorrow was the start of a new adventure!

It was the morning that Violet was to leave and the sky was clear and the sun was just showing on the horizon with a wonderful array of colours. Violet got on the stagecoach with three other people and they set off, with two horses pulling and a driver and a footman. The people on the coach introduced themselves, telling one another who they were, what business they were on and where they were going. When Violet told them her plan, one of the travellers, an old lady with bright blue eyes and a dark blue hooded cape with a dark red velvet trim, had found it rather interesting. The other two, however, thought it quite mad! That evening the stagecoach arrived at the coaching inn for a rest stop. "Only one more day travelling," Violet thought to herself.

The next morning came soon enough, and the travelling companions were back on the stagecoach again. There was only Violet and one other person on the stagecoach this time, it was the old lady from the day before.

"Hello again my dear," said the old lady warmly, "tell me more about your planting along the highway and byways of these well travelled roads."

"Well, it all started when I was a little girl," Violet replied, "I was on a long journey with my parents, when the cart we were riding in shed a wheel. We had to stay with the cart under a canvas overnight and we had nothing to eat. It was then that I thought, 'if only there was an apple tree nearby or maybe a pear tree, it would be so welcoming.'

So that's about it really. About this time of year every year, I go around planting things that can be eaten."

The old lady thought for a moment and said,

"Well my dear, that is most lovely of you. You are one of life's givers and not a taker like so many people."

"I don't understand?" replied Violet.

"What I mean my dear, is that you give something back to the world. Helping others, rather than take, take, take as some folk would do!" the old lady explained.

"Oh, I see," said Violet, "that's so kind of you to say!"

It was early afternoon and Violet was looking out the window, when she saw a nice opening in the hedgerow coming up on the next corner. She called to the driver,

"Do we have time to stop?"

"Yes," replied the driver, "but five minutes mind, that is all."

Violet quickly pulled a small spade from her pack and a tree and jumped out of the stagecoach. As she did so, she turned to the driver and said,

"I just need to plant something."

Violet started digging.

"You can't do it there!" The driver exclaimed. He had thought that it was quite something else that Violet was in need of! Violet suddenly realised what the driver had thought and blushed a little.

"No no, it's fine, I am only planting a plum tree here."

"A what?" said the driver.

"A plum tree." Violet replied.

"Why would you want to stop and plant a plum tree?" asked the driver, quite puzzled.

"Well, if you should pass along here some day and shed a wheel, there will always be something to eat should you have to wait a long time for help to arrive."

The driver could think of nothing to reply to that, but thought she was quite mad!

Violet did finish her adventure of planting trees and other plants that bore fruit or could be eaten and for many more years, she did the same all over the country.

So if you happen to be out walking, down some old well trodden lane and you see some random apple or plum trees, or perhaps patches of strawberries or garlic growing in the middle of nowhere, it may once have been the main route to a village or a town long ago. Perhaps it was even Violet herself who had planted them there!

But now you know how it came to be there.

MAGGIE

Maggie was a happy go lucky young woman who would always see the best in everything. In autumn she would step outside of her little cottage and say,
"Oh look at the beautiful leaves, see how they fall floating and fluttering down to the ground," even though it was raining. Even that in itself was beautiful to Maggie as she would say,
"Oh how the rain looks like little jewels shaped like teardrops, falling to our feet and painting our way with shimmering splendor."

Winter came, but to Maggie it was with a carpet of beautiful frost that covered everywhere with glitter that soon faded in the winter sun. When the winter's cold bite would draw in, Maggie's mother would say,
"The wind is so cold, it cuts through you like a knife," and Maggie would look at her mother and say,
"Well mother, we will have to wrap up and snuggle together by the fire, that's what we must do. The fire with its flames all aglow with golds and reds, will make our faces quite rosy."

Snow had started to fall and Maggie would rush outside to watch it flutter down so delicately. As she watched each flake gently fall, she would cry,
"How beautiful," turning around and around with her arms outstretched catching the odd snowflake in her hands and watching it melt away.

People from the village where Maggie lived would often try to catch her attention, just to hear what she had to say, as they found her words quite warming or even calming. Her words seemed to chase any worries that they might have away.

One day Maggie was outside, taking in the beauty of the world, when an old man pushing a small cart passed by. He was a stranger to Maggie for he was not from the village. The old man was cursing his life, not very happy with his lot and having to push a heavy cart full of his trade to be delivered to some of the houses in the village.

Maggie went to the garden gate and said,
"Good morning sir, what a beautiful day it is today."
The old man stopped and before he spoke, looked around at the day to see just how wonderful it was meant to be.
"What is so wonderful about this day?" he replied gruffly.
"Oh just look at the clouds drifting over the hills, the trees swaying in the wind so gracefully and that lovely lady all snuggled into her shawl."
"Huh, the clouds are grey as is much of the sky, the trees are going back and forth because it is windy and the lady has got to wrap up as it is so cold." the old man replied.

Maggie's mother had come out to see where Maggie had got to and had stumbled into most of the conversation.

"Oh yes, but can you not see the beauty in that? Look again, see how the clouds move, how the trees dance and the wonderful image that meets your eyes at that moment with the lady wrapped in her shawl." said Maggie.
The old man looked around, first up to the clouds then to the trees, although by now the lady had gone.
"Well," said the old man, "if you put it like that, I suppose I do."
The old man turned to Maggie's mother and said,
"Is your daughter always like this, so in awe of everything?"
"Oh yes, she has always seen the best in everything." Maggie's

mother replied warmly. The old man turned to Maggie,
"Well, you have certainly brightened up my day!" With that, the old man picked up his cart and walked on, but now with a smile on his face.
"Well, that old man certainly seemed to be very grumpy to start with," said Maggie's mother to her, "but now he's Smiling. How very lovely!"
"I think perhaps he has had a hard life and hasn't had time to see the beauty in what was around him, but now I think he might."

Later that day, a young lad and his mother from the village were passing by and saw Maggie still standing by the garden gate. They went over to talk to her, as they felt that perhaps they too could do with some of Maggie's lust for life. The young lads mother said,
"What do you make of the day Maggie, it's a bit cold, isn't it?"
For once, Maggie could not think of a word to say, as her eyes were fixed on the young lad and all she could think of was what wonderful eyes he had and how lovely his hair was, shining like threads of dark silk. Maggie had known the young lad growing up, she went to school with him, but had never seen him in this way before as a few years had now passed.

Maggie tried to answer,
"Yes, well, er, it's a fine day." she stuttered. The lads' mother looked surprised and asked,
"That's not like you Maggie, you usually tell of how wonderful everything is, even on the darkest of days."
Maggie gathered her senses,
"Oh, well yes," she said, then clearing her throat managed to tell of how lovely the drifting clouds were rolling over the hills and of the trees dancing to the rhythm of the wind, with the fallen leaves chasing one another and the games they were playing.
Maggie then turned to the young lad, and said,
"What about you, what do you find lovely about a day?"
The young lad turned to look at Maggie with his dark eyes and after some thought he said,

"I love the sunrise, the sunset and everything in between."
Maggie's heart skipped and as she stared into the young lad's eyes, Maggie knew she had never felt like this before.

"Maybe you would like to talk some more about the wonderful world in which we live and about the beauty that is in reach of our fingertips, right there just in front of us."

Maggie stood still, a slight blush rising on her cheeks and words failing her, but eventually she managed to blurt out,

"Yes I would."

From that day until this, Maggie and that young lad are still together, even though they are now grey and old, but still holding

hands. Every day, they still tell and show one another new and wonderful things in the world and delight in how beautiful each day is, no matter what it brings.

Maybe we should all be a little bit more Maggie, by just stopping once in a while and looking to see the beauty in the world around us.

THE WISHING WELL

A very long time ago when wells were dug, in the time when human people and fairy folk lived in harmony, the well was not just a place to draw water from, it was also a gateway to the fairy world. It was not for people to pass through but somewhere for humans to buy their wishes.

Each well had a well guardian. These guardians were one of the fairy folk that would process the wishes of the human people. Should the person's wish be for wealth, then it would not be granted, as this would make the human people lazy. Most other wishes were granted though, as long as a coin that was thrown into the well and that each coin had its own worth!

As the years passed the wells were all but forgotten about until one day when one of the wells and its guardian was awoken.

John and Dot were great friends, they lived quite close to each other in the same village. They had known each other since they were born as their mothers had befriended one another before John and Dot were born. There was only six weeks between the two of them in age, Dot being the older.

John had gone around to see Dot, and he cheerfully knocked on her front door. The door opened and it was Dot's mother who answered.

"Hello John,"said Dot's mother, "Dot is out the back in the garden, go through."

John went through the house to the back door and into the garden shouting,

"Hey!"

"Hoe!" shouted Dot back.

"Are you up too much today?" asked John.

"Nothing much" Dot replied, "just got to tidy up out here then I'm done."

"Got anything you want to do after you have finished? I can give you a hand if you like?" John began rolling his sleeves up.

"We could throw stones at the cans again?" sighed Dot.

"We did that yesterday and the day before! Oh what is there to do in this village?" sighed John back.

"I know, how about we go up to the copse and build camps!"

"Oh yes!" replied Dot with more enthusiasm.

John helped tidy up the garden then told Dot's mother where they were going. The two of them set off along the village road. On the way there they passed the village green and by the green there was an old well. It was a shabby looking thing with a tiled roof over it and it hadn't been used for years. All the village folk called it the wishing well.

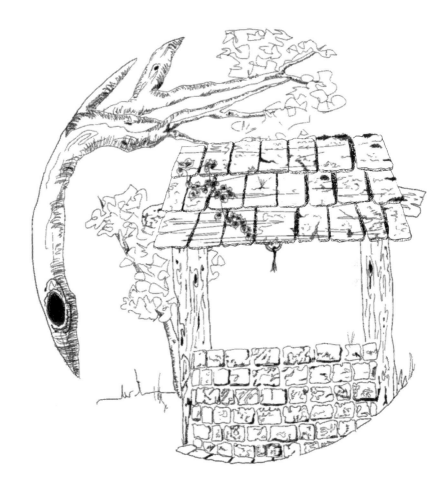

As John and Dot went past, John said,
"I'm going to make a wish!"
"What are you going to wish for John?"
"Well," John replied, then continued, "I am going to wish for this village to be more interesting."
"That sounds like a great idea." laughed Dot.
John took a small coin out of his pocket, held it over the well and said,
"I wish this village was more interesting!" He let go of the coin and 'plop', it fell into the well water.

John and Dot carried on to the copse. First they decided to build a camp for Dot, propping poles and sticks against a tree, then covering it with leaves and leaving a little opening at the side. John picked some wild flowers and passed them to Dot saying,

"There you go my lady, something to make your camp more pretty."
"Well, thank you kind Sir." giggled Dot, then did a little curtsy in a joking kind of manner.
Next they built a camp much the same as Dots, for John, but the door was on the other side of his camp, so that the door on both camps faced each other. Then John made a spear and said,
"This is to keep wild animals away!"

Dot and John had enough of camp building and decided to head back home. They walked back down the road to the village and passed the village green and the well. John ran over to the well and shouted,
"The village is still not interesting!"
As he turned back to face Dot, John nearly jumped out of his skin, for in front of him was not Dot but instead a small man with strange facial features.
The man's face was very wrinkly. John hadn't seen this man in the village before, he was sure he would have remembered. The man smiled, and said,
"Did you make a wish, lad?"
"Er, yes" stammered John. The small man continued saying,
"It's no good making a wish these days, your coins are just a token, they are not real. There is no worth in your coins now and you can't wish with a token! Old coins were made of real silver that had a value that you could wish with."
John rubbed his eyes and when he opened them again, there was Dot right back in front of him.
"Are you alright?" enquired Dot, "you look like you've seen a ghost."
"Or perhaps worse." John replied. John explained what had happened.

"Well I didn't see anyone and I was here all the time." Dot thought John was pulling her leg!

John felt unsure about what he had seen, it had seemed so clear, but now he was starting to doubt himself. John said goodbye to Dot as they got to her house and he walked on, still thinking about what that little strange man had said.

John went into his house, found his mother and asked her, "Have the coins we use changed from the olden day coins?"

"What do you mean? Do you mean what are they called?" questioned his mother.

"No, I mean what coins are made of, like silver?"

"Oh I don't know," replied his mother, "but there is a little box full of old coins in the dresser, you could have a look and see? I'm not sure how you will be able to tell what they are made of though."

John took the box from the dresser drawer and when he opened it, there were thrupenny bits, sixpences, shillings, half crowns, farthings and great big penny pieces inside.

John then went up to his bedroom where he found a magnet. He opened his money jar, took his magnet and plopped it into the jar. When he pulled it out there were coins stuck all over it. John pulled the coins off and put them back in his coin jar, then dropped the magnet into the old coin box. When he then pulled the magnet out of the box, not one coin stuck to it.

John went back down to his mother and said, "They are made of something quite different, new coins are magnetic, old coins aren't. Please can I have one of the old coins?"

"Yes of course, I have no need for them."

John reached into the box and pulled out a sixpence, then ran back to the well and held his hand, still clutching the sixpence, over the opening of the well.

"Please, I wish for this village to be more interesting," his voice echoed around the deep well and then he dropped the coin, 'plop'. As it fell into the well water, it looked as if tiny little sparks flew up the well shaft. John then walked back home, crossing his fingers for extra luck.

The next day a fair set up on the village green, there had never been a fair in the village ever before.

Dot ran around to John's house,
"Have you seen John? Have you seen there is a fair, A FAIR!" she cried breathlessly.

From that day on there was always something most interesting going on in that village and John and Dot enjoyed every day of it.

If you ever find an old well and you want to make a wish, make sure you throw something of worth down that well, for your wish might just come true!

STOP TIME

There once was a boy called Tom, who did not want to grow old, for he had seen what age had done to his grandparents and even his parents. How they complained of aches and pains, how slow it had made old folks that he knew and how often they would say to him,

"Oh you don't want to get old, my boy!"

Tom thought to himself,

"If I and I alone could stop time itself, then I wouldn't get any older."

Now his first thoughts turned to the clocks, as he could hear time passing away with every 'tick, tick, tick'.

"What if I were to stop the clock, perhaps that would that be enough to hold time back?" Tom thought to himself. Tom decided that on this very day, he would stop the biggest clock in the house. The biggest clock in the house was an old Grandfather clock, that stood grandly, towering above everything else in the hall, always making that same noise, 'tick, tick, tick'.

Tom went to the old clock, looked at it up and down and saw a clear door under the clock face. He opened it and there he could see a big pendulum swinging back and forth with every 'tick, tick, tick'.

Tom put his hand in and stopped the pendulum swinging. He stood still and listened and could no longer hear that 'tick, tick, tick'.

"Do I feel like I have stopped getting older?" he thought, but he really couldn't tell.

Tom's father came out of the living room, down the hall and past the old grandfather clock. He noticed that it had stopped as he could no longer hear that .tick, tick, tick'.

Tom's father asked Tom's mother,

"Has the grandfather clock been wound up this morning?"

"Yes, of course dear" replied Tom's mother.

"Well that's strange, it seems to have stopped." Tom's father said, as he gazed at the clock.

Tom was still standing by the old grandfather clock wondering if he had stopped ageing. Both Tom's parents were now looking at the old big clock and Tom's father turned and looked at Tom with a puzzled look on his face.

"The grandfather clock has stopped working."

"I know," said Tom, "I did it, for I want to stop time itself."

"Why would you want to stop time?" asked his father.

"Well if I can stop time, I will not grow old and have aches and pains or become slow like the old folks."

"That might be true," said Tom's father, "but all you have done is stopped us from telling the time. The day will still turn to night and that will be another day gone."

Tom's father opened the door on the old grandfather clock and set the pendulum swinging again. He then took out his pocket watch and set the old clock to the right time. 'Tick, tick, tick', the old grandfather clock went.

Tom looked at his father, now he with a puzzled face, and said,

"If I could stop day turning into night. Would that stop time?"

His father stopped and thought for a while.

"Well, to stop day turning into night you would have to stop the world from turning. Then for all time it would be day or night depending on where you stopped it. I think perhaps we should go and visit the old professor. You could ask him how you could stop time, for he has great wisdom and knows so much of things like that."

Tom's father took him to see the old professor. They walked up to the wooden door and knocked. The door slowly opened and there stood the old professor, with a long grey beard, a funny round hat that looked like it was made of fine carpet and a long embroidered housecoat of dark red and green with gold braiding down the seams.

"Hello," said the old professor, "and how can I help you on this very fine day?"

Tom's father explained everything to the old professor.

"Come in, come in. Now, my dear boy, you want to stop time itself?"

"Yes." replied Tom.

"Well, time should not be stopped, for if we could, or indeed did, all life as we know so far would also stop. Grain in the field would not ripen and then would not be able to be harvested. The fruit on the trees would not form, and the hen would have no more chicks and in turn there would be no more eggs. Our knowledge would also not grow, for each generation gives ideas that inspire others and those ideas are built on and improved by each new generation. For time itself is life and we must make the most of the time we have. We can only make it our own time and this time is our time! It will always move on and it will continue to do so, with or without the 'tick, tick, tick', my dear boy!"

As Tom grew up, he was so inspired by the old professor and he studied hard. He wanted to go to university and carry on learning, so that one day he too might inspire others and that he could make a difference in this world. Even though he could not stop time and he too one day will get old with aches and pains, Toms name could live forever, through the great things he might achieve!

THE BLANKET
OF DREAMS

Once, long ago, there was a boy whose name was Jake and Jake could not sleep. It was a week and a day since their old dog had died and Jake had played and loved that dog growing up. He had always been with Jake, as the dog was only a puppy when Jake was born.

Jake lived in a small village that was a long way from the nearest town. If they had a horse, it would have been a day's ride there and a day's ride back. Jake's mother decided to see an old lady that lived in a little cottage on the edge of the great forest and to ask her advice on how to help Jake sleep.

Jake's mother went to the mantelpiece over the old, black , iron kitchen stove and picked up a little wooden box. She took out the last silver sixpence that she had left, that lay within and put on her shawl and set off. Out of the village she went and over the sty that lay between a neatly laid hedge and out across the meadow. The wind had been blowing all day and it nearly took the shawl off her shoulders. Jake's mother had wondered why she had bothered to put the shawl on at all as it had offered no warmth on that early spring day.

Jake's mother arrived at the old lady's cottage, with the great forest looming in the background and opened the gate. The cottage garden was surrounded by a wattled hazel fence. Just as Jake's mother stepped into the old ladies garden, the wind had gone! She noticed that the garden was full of plants and herbs, some of which she didn't recognise. She walked up to the little cottage door,knocked on it and after a while, the door slowly opened with a long sounding 'creek'. There stood a little old lady, no more than four feet high, with a smile on her weathered wrinkled face.

"Hello my dear, what brings you to my door?" said the little old lady.

"Please, if you don't mind, I need your help and wisdom." Then Jake's mother explained about Jake not having slept for a week and a day.

As Jake's mother finished telling the old lady about him, a bright twinkle appeared in her piercing blue eyes.

"Well my dear, I have just the thing for such an ailment." she said and went off into another room. There she got a large box from a cupboard with many shelves, each full of different boxes and jars.

"Here you are my dear," and the old lady passed a blanket to Jake's mother and said, "this is the blanket of dreams. This will make the lad sleep, for it is woven from flax, with jasmine to help him relax, valerian to induce sleep and lavender to give him a deeper sleep. It was all spun on a walnut spinning wheel that is rubbed with beeswax after each spool of thread is cast."

"Will it work?" thought Jake's mother, but wasn't brave enough to say it.

"It will work my dear." said the old lady. Jake's mother was taken aback by this as she had only thought it and not said it out loud!

"You must also make a tea with camomile and sweeten it with two spoons of honey," the old lady said.

"Thank you so much," Jake's mother said, "but I'm afraid that I don't have any camomile for the tea."

"Well my dear! Let's see what I can find." and the old lady went to her kitchen, opened a pot and tipped out some camomile onto a big brown leaf. The leaf was soft and supple, not dry and crispy as Jake's mother would have expected it to be. The old lady gathered the leaf together and tied it at the top, like a pouch, with a piece of raffia twine.

"When you are done with the blanket you must bring it back to me!" The old lady said softly.

"Oh yes of course," Jake's mother said, "I must pay you," and held out her hand with the silver sixpence.

"Oh no, I will not take any money, all I ask is that you might give me anything you may have that is surplus to your needs. Candle stumps, apples that will no longer store, a hen that will no longer lay? You know, that sort of thing."

All these things Jake's mother had, a box of old candle stumps, a drawer full of apples from last Autumn that would not keep much longer and one of the chickens had indeed stopped laying. 'How would the old lady know this?' Jake's mother thought, but she was pleased with the bargain as could keep their last silver sixpence.

So again, Jake's mother thanked the old lady and left the little cottage through the garden and out of the gate and as soon as she had shut the gate, there it was again, that wind!

She walked through the meadow back to the village and home.

Jake was not looking well. He had a hollow look about him, his eyes were bloodshot and he was so pale.

Jake's mother made him the camomile tea and put in the two spoons of honey.

Jake drank the tea after it had cooled a little, then took the blanket to bed. He lay down, shuffled about for a bit until he was comfortable and pulled the blanket of dreams up half way over his face, with just his eyes peeping out over the top.

His mother came to see how he was doing and she saw that he was soon off to the land of nod.

Two days had passed and Jake had not woken and his mother was getting worried, so she pulled the blanket off his face.

The next day, Jake awoke. Jake's mother and father were having breakfast at their kitchen table. Jake walked into the kitchen and said,

"Morning!"

"Hello," said his mother, "how are you feeling?"

"I feel fantastic," replied Jake. "I've been with the dog. We played so many games! we were over by the edge of the great forest and all the time we were playing. Even now when I shut my eyes, I'm back there, with that naughty playful dog!"

From that day until Jake was old and passed away, Jake would play with that dog in his dreams and he always slept very well!

◆ ◆ ◆

THE ENCHANTED LAND

T here once was a time when human people and fairy folk lived in peaceful harmony, crossing into each other's worlds quite freely. But then one day, a new king came to the throne and he was obsessed with conquering and combining other kingdoms, so that his own empire became bigger and more powerful.

As his kingdom grew and grew, the king still wasn't satisfied and wanted even more powerful things and he thought that the fairy folk had just such things.

Although human people could cross over into the enchanted land and the fairy folk into our world, neither would interfere with the other's business.

Whereas human people would war against each other, fairy folk did not, they were very much at peace with one another.

The fairy folk could live for a very long time and had magic, so really they had everything they needed. None of the land in which they lived was owned by any one fairy, elf, pixie or sprite, but instead they had a council of elders to keep order should things get out of hand, though they hardly ever did.

The king was very envious of the fairy folk, he wanted to live for a very long time and to have their magic. For he believed that if he had their magic, he could rule the whole of the human world. He thought that with magic, every battle would be easier for him to win and if he had a much longer life then he would have time to conquer everywhere and more time to enjoy the rewards.

The king's envy grew and grew. He simply must have the fairy magic, but he knew he could not get it by declaring war against the fairy folk, for they had magic and could slow down human time and the power to speed theirs up.

The fairy folk could cut all the bow strings before an archer could load the bow with arrows. They could turn all the swords into dust at the click of fingers, but aside from that, fairy folk had the best archers you could find anywhere. They never missed their targets!

The king decided that he would go and speak with the council of elders and persuade them to let him have the fairy folk magic.

The king gathered some of his best men, and rode into the enchanted land. Once there, the king saw an elf sitting on a rock, staring back at the group of riders.

The king called out in a most commanding voice,

"I want to spark with your elders."

"You can't," replied the elf, "they don't sit until the next full moon."

The king flew into a rage just like that and said,

"I want to see them now!"

The elf suddenly disappeared from sight, found a thin willow stick and whipped the king's ear with it.

"Ow!" cried the king but before he could say anything else, the elf laughed and replied,

"You can't till the next full moon," then the elf vanished again!

"I'm going to gut that sprite," shouted the king "it's more than a week away till the full moon, I'm not waiting that long!"

The king and his men rode on until they found a little cottage. The king ordered one of his men to knock on the cottage door and a tiny old woman opened it and said, "How can I help you?"

"I demand to see the council of elders." replied the king.

"Oh no, I'm afraid you can't," replied the tiny old woman, "they don't sit until the next full moon." The king's face went red, then purple and finally blue with anger! The tiny old woman said,
"It's no use getting upset dear, you will simply have to wait and besides, you will have to let them know that you are coming."
"How am I going to do that, if I can't speak to them?"
The tiny old woman replied,
"Why, you must write them a letter of course."
"And who am I supposed to give it to and where am I supposed to send it?" said the king.
"You don't give it to anyone," the old woman laughed, "you just burn it and then you get your reply."
"What?" shouted the king. The tiny woman replied, speaking very slowly this time,
"You just burn it! Do you have ink and parchment?" The king and all his men looked at each other in amazement and shrugged their shoulders.
"Here, I will get you some," and she went back into the cottage and returned with a quill and parchment, then handed it to the king. The king wrote the letter asking for a meeting and handed it back to the tiny old woman. She took the letter from him and put it on her fire. The letter went up in flames. It turned black with hundreds of bright glowing sparks all over and then the letter broke up and the sparks flew up the chimney.
The tiny old woman said,
"There, it has been sent, you will have a reply soon," and closed the door in the king's face!
The king and his men turned around then rode back home in total silence, for they did not know what to say.

The next day a letter appeared on the king's desk! No one had delivered it, it had just appeared there, but it was from the fairy folk's council of elders, naming a time and place of the next full moon.
The day before the next full moon, the king and some of his men rode off once more for the enchanted land, to meet with the fairy folk elders.

The king stood in front of the council of elders and said that he wanted their magic and he needed a long life, as the human world would be all the better for it.

The elders spoke to each other, in a language that the king did not understand, then one of the elders stood up and said,

"This will never happen, it is written in the law of the stones. It is because of the greed of man, that humans shall not possess magic or a long life, or indeed anything from our world. Your people have wiped out giants, trolls, orcs and the dragons are all but gone from your world, what shall it be next? The wolves and bears?"

"But they attacked us." cried the king.

"They only attacked because you did not let them live on the land that they had a right to. The law stones also warn that if humans ever did get magic, they would want the enchanted lands too and there would be nothing to stop them."

"The answer is most definitely no!" called another of the elders.

The king flew into such a rage. He threatened the fairy folk that should they ever come into the human world again, he would kill them all and from that day magic was to be banned in the human world.

The king stormed off, shouting and kicking at whatever he could, be it the ground or a rock.

The council carried on with their meeting and came to the decision that all the gateways must be closed between the enchanted land from the human world.

The gateways have stayed closed ever since, but because fairy folk live such a long time, they can still remember that day!

Mind you, it doesn't stop them coming into our world to play tricks on the human people occasionally and sometimes a gateway might even be left open!

◆ ◆ ◆

BETWEEN TWO WORLDS

D aniel was a young lad, and like most young lads, loved to be out exploring the world where he lived.

One day, when Daniel was exploring the stream at the bottom of their garden, Daniel's father called after him,
"Tomorrow my boy, I want you to come with me. You need to learn a trade, for you are now of an age when you need to earn your keep".
Daniel's father was a woodsman working in the forest, selecting diseased and dying trees that needed to be taken out. The rest were left to grow and mature for the landlord.
Daniel's fathers only income was what he could get from the timber he sold. It was not a great income, but it was a living and the family were happy enough.

The next day, Daniel went with his father to where he was to be working
and he watched as his father took down a dead tree. Daniel's father said,
"This is only good for firewood, my boy. Hodgkins will pick this up on Wednesday, with the rest of the firewood."
Hodgkins sold firewood, he brought the dead wood and branches that were no good for anything else off Daniel's father.

Just as many other young lads do, Daniel's mind started to wander as he walked a little further into the forest and it was not long before he came across a large beech tree with a large hollow trunk.

"That's strange." Daniel thought to himself, for he had noticed that above the opening to the hollow in the tree was some strange writing.

Daniel peered into the hollow,

"This looks interesting," he thought, "I wonder how far up it is hollow?"

As he clambered through the opening, to look up, he found that he was immediately back on the outside looking straight back at the tree. Daniel shook himself to make quite sure he was not daydreaming.

"The wind must be just playing tricks with my eyes" he said, as when he looked back at the opening he noticed the writing was no longer above the door.

Daniel looked around, everything looked different. There were trees that he had not seen before, he was quite sure. The sky was no longer dull and overcast with clouds, it was a clear sky that was a pinky blue, not like the blue that he knew of on a clear day. Daniel walked a little way but he did not want to lose sight of the tree. 'Zip'! Something flew right past him and he was sure he could hear laughing as it went by.

"Hello, is there anybody there?"

Daniel was a little nervous by now and started going back towards the tree. Suddenly a hedgehog dashed out in front of him. He stopped, the hedgehog stopped, looked at Daniel, raised its eyes and tutted. With that, Daniel made for the tree as quickly as he could!

Daniel clambered inside the tree, but no sooner was he in, he found himself back outside of the hollow again, looking at the same opening, but this time, the writing was back, where he had seen it before, above the hollow opening.

Daniel was relieved to be back, but at the same time could not help thinking,

"Did that hedgehog really just tut at me?"

"I wondered where you had got to!" It was Daniel's father. Daniel was sure now that he must have been day dreaming!

That evening Daniel's father asked him,

"Well what was it like then?"

"What?" replied Daniel,startled.

"what was what like?"

"Your first day working of course, although I'm not sure what work you did?" said Daniel's father.

"Err, oh yes, great, it was great. I will come with you again tomorrow." Daniel replied.

"Good boy," said his father and went off to his bed.

The following day Daniel and his father went back to the forest, where they had been the day before, but as soon as they arrived, Daniel had things on his mind other than work!

Daniel's father was busy selecting bits of oak that were just the right length and had no knots in. They were too small to send to the sawmill, but this wood was perfect for making the pegs that hold timber framed buildings together. Daniel's father would sit and make these pegs on really wet days, when it was too wet to work in the forest, or sometimes in the evenings, sat by the fire.

Daniel's father started to explain to him how to make the pegs.

"Well my boy," he said, "this is an art. The pegs have to be tapered down just so, then a point is cut in. You need to have eight sides going around the peg, so when you look at it from the top, it.... Where has he gone now?" he said to himself as he could no longer see his son.

Daniel had slipped away, back to the tree with the hollow. He clambered back through the hollow opening just as he had done the day before, back to see if there really had been a strange land after all.

Once through, he saw two butterflies that fluttered around him. He had not seen their like before, on any of his adventures into the woods and they were certainly very different to the ones he knew. Daniel was sure they were looking him up and down, as if they too had not seen his like before. Daniel wandered further away from the tree this time, where he saw some strange flowers growing, again like nothing he had ever seen before. He bent his head down to smell them to see if they had a scent, but as his head got closer to the flowers, they moved away!

"This is a very strange place!" thought Daniel. He then had the funniest feeling that something was watching him. Daniel pretended to look at the ground, whilst looking out the corner of his eye. There! He could just make out two figures watching him, hiding in a bush. They looked no more than two feet high.

"They can't be children?" Daniel thought, "not out on their own?" for they could only be about two or three years old at the most.

Suddenly, there was a loud crack, then a smashing sound. It had come from the direction of the tree he had just come out of.

Daniel looked at the bush where he had seen the two figures, they were now gone. Terrified, Daniel ran back to the tree and scrabbled back through the hollow opening.

"Where the devil have you been?" It was Daniel's father, with a very worried look on his face.

No longer was Daniel looking at the tree with the hollow opening and the writing over it, for it was now laying on the forest floor. Daniel's father had cut it down.

Daniel realised that he had not properly come back through the opening, he had passed out of the other world but not fully back into this one. Daniel was now inbetween worlds. He could still see his father, but his voice sounded muffled and quiet. He could still see the flowers that he had tried to sniff, from the other world. He went over to them and ran his hands through them. This time they did not move out of his hands way and he could not feel them in his fingers, it was almost as if he wasn't there.

"What are you doing boy!" called his father.

"The flowers" replied Daniel.

"What flowers," said his father, "and why does your voice sound strange, it sounds almost like you are far away and it has an echo?"

Daniel explained as best he could as to what had happened, and all that he had seen. Something was flying around Daniel, he put his hand up to touch it, but he couldn't feel it. Daniel's father couldn't see what Daniel was trying to touch. He looked at his son, but Daniel had a far away, glazed look to his eyes and he could not focus on his father. It was almost as though he was looking right through him.

"Oh, what are we to do my boy, what are we to do?" Daniel's father said, almost in tears.

"I can't put the tree back up where it was!"

Daniel and his father both sat down in despair with their heads in their hands.

Suddenly, Daniel heard a voice. He looked up and there in front of him stood a man in a long cloak, with a hood pulled up so that it covered his face. Daniel could just make out strange markings on the man's face.

The strange man said,

"Daniel, you cannot put the tree back, but you can put the door back, it must be exactly in the same place." Then, as quick as that, the man was gone.

"Father we must cut the tree off, just above the strange writing above the opening. Then we must put it back on the stump in exactly the same place. Only then can I return to you."

Daniel's father picked up his saw and cut the tree off, just above the writing, as Daniel had instructed. However, when it was cut through, the trunk was far too heavy to lift.

"What are we to do?" said Daniel's father.

"Could we cut it in half top to bottom with the doorway untouched?"

"No," said his father, "it would split above the doorway from the weight either side, but I do have an idea."

Daniel's father carefully made several marks on the tree, then cut halfway through each, from behind the door. He then picked up his hammer and wedge, splitting out the half rings and leaving the top and bottom rings above and below the door still in place. That will keep it from splitting, said Daniel's father.

Now they could finally lift it up and shuffle it back onto the stump, getting it in exactly the right place.
Daniel wasted no time, he lept through the opening and disappeared. Once he was on the other side, he clambered back through the opening and reappeared all to his fathers amazement.
"Well?" said his father.
"It's not worked," cried Daniel, desperately. His father knew straight away that it had not worked, for as soon as his son spoke, he still had a distant voice with the echo sound, just as before..
"Try again, only try more slowly through this time." said his father. Daniel did just that, but still no change. Daniel cried,
"I am stuck like this forever! Neither in this world or in that!"
Daniel's father thought quickly,
"I have an idea, go around the back of the tree and climb through that way. Daniel went around to the back of the tree, stepped up on to the stump, through where his father had cut out the half rings and back through the opening from inside the tree. Immediately Daniel shouted,
"Yes, yes!" and fell on his knees, with tears rolling down his face.
"I'm back!" he cried.
Daniel's father knocked down the doorway off the stump and smashed it up, saying "Never again will you, nor anyone else get stuck in between worlds."

Or will they? For if you see someone talking to themselves or reaching up as if to touch something that isn't there, be kind, as they may be stuck inbetween two worlds and can't find their way back!

THE WOLF

Before stories were written down, they were only told by word of mouth, passed down through generations long ago in the dawn of mankind.

There lived a family, surviving from hunting and gathering. Their home was nothing more than the animal skins that they had hunted, stretched over a wooden frame. They were simple structures that could easily be moved to follow the herds of aurochs; large wild cattle and giant elk. These animals were much bigger than the cattle we have today and it would take the family a lot of effort to hunt them.

Hunting was becoming harder and harder for the family. The children, a boy and a girl were not quite in their teens and were not yet strong enough to hunt for days. Their father was a strong and fit man, but their grandfather was old and very much slower.
The mother and grandmother would lead the group that went out each day to forage for berries, dig roots for food and maybe if they were lucky and it was the right time of year, collect eggs from nests. Food from hunting animals was getting scarce and it seemed the same for other hunting animals like the wolf.

One day a young wolf came close to the camp searching for food. The adults tried driving it away, but it insisted on hanging around. "Be careful," said the father, "it may attack you if it sees that you are on your own."

For days the wolf stayed close to the camp, never coming too near. On one of these days, the boy threw a piece of dry meat for the wolf, who ate it gladly. Then the girl did the same. " No!" said the mother, "Don't give our food to the wolf for there will be none left for us!"

As the days went on, the two children sneaked out small bits of meat for the wolf, without the parents or the grandparents knowing.

The wolf was getting closer and closer to the camp each day, but it was still very timid.

One night the family were woken by an awful noise of growls and snarls.They jumped up to see what was making such a terrifying noise. They could see the wolf fighting with a bear and then chasing it away.

The grandfather spoke, saying how good it was that the wolf had been there to chase the bear away.

"Who knows what might have happened if the bear had got into the camp, one of us might have been badly hurt or even killed!"

The next morning the wolf was not to be seen hanging around like it usually did. The girl and boy had set out to collect firewood, when they found the wolf laying down injured from the fight from the bear. The wolf could hardly move, so the boy and girl stretched an animal skin over two poles and carried the wolf back to the home camp, to treat the wounds.

The boy and girl spent quite a few days nursing the wolf's wounds and feeding it until it was fully recovered.

One day the father said to the girl and boy, " You two must come hunting with me as grandfather can no longer keep up. He will still be coming, but will have to catch up with us later."

After a while the girl noticed the wolf was following them. They spotted aurochs and tracked and chased one for hours. Then a strange thing happened! They noticed the wolf was also helping with the hunt, stopping the animal from turning and forcing it to go straight. When they thought they had lost it, the wolf picked up its scent and chased it out into the open again, it somehow knew how to hunt with people, almost reading their thoughts of directions. Finally they caught it.

The family let the wolf have some of the aurochs meat before taking it back to their home camp.

The girl said, "We would not have caught that if the wolf had not come with us."

"You're right!" the father replied.

"I have not seen anything like that in all my days. From where I was, I could see the wolf working with you, as if knowing every move it should make!" the grandfather exclaimed in disbelief.

As the days went by, the family made more hunting trips and each time they were very successful too. Then the wolf disappeared for a few days and the family had no idea where the wolf had gone, but ten weeks later the wolf gave birth to six pups, right there in the camp.

The family helped raise the pups by bringing food to the wolf and then to the pups as they grew.

After a while when the pups had grown into young wolves, they too helped with the hunts. Soon, other people saw the family hunting with the wolves, that not only hunted, but gave protection from other people trying to raid their food. The wolves also helped by keeping bears and other wolves away.

When the young wolves had pups of their own, the wolf pups started to change. Their coats got darker and their ears started to stand a little less up right.

Ever since then people have always been with the wolf as we are today with our dogs and they are all descended from the european grey wolf and nothing more.

WHEN THE NIGHT
CLOSES IN

D aisy was a worrier. She always had been since she was
quite little. Daisy had grown into a lovely young teenager.
Daisy was fine in the day, nothing seemed to bother her at
all, but when the night closed in, then things seemed very different.

One day Daisy's father had hurt his shoulder while working and
he could no longer lift his arm up as it sent pains across his shoulder and down his back.

Daisy had not thought anything about it during the day. That
night however, when darkness had fallen and she was all alone in
her bed, thoughts crept into Daisy's head, picking at the threads of
sensibility and unraveling any reasonable thought.

Daisy could not sleep thinking of her poor fathers shoulder. What
if he could not work? What would happen to them, how could
they live? With no money to buy food, where would they go?

Daisy got up. She paced up and down for a bit, hoping it would
clear her thoughts, it didn't.

"Mum, Mum," she called. Daisy's mother came to her,

"What is it, my love?"

"Im worried about Dad, will he be alright? Will we lose the cottage? How will we eat if we can't buy anything? Should I give up

school and find work? Will he ever be able to work again?"

Her mother quickly stopped Daisy's gabbling,

"Hold on there my love, so many questions! Stop worrying, it's only the night terrors getting the better of you. You know your father, when has anything ever stopped him? He will be as right as rain once he has had a nice hot bath."

"Now get yourself into that bed and I will tell you something that will take your mind off it."

Daisy's mother tucked her back into bed, then brushed the hair gently away from Daisy's face with her hand and said,

"Do you remember when you were little and you went to bed, you would say, 'Is there something in the wardrobe?' I would have to go and look. I looked and would say, 'no there is nothing in here.' then you would say, 'Can you check under the bed? ' and I would kneel down to have a look. I would say, 'there is nothing there,' and you would say, 'have you looked properly?' and I would say, 'yes.'"

"This is all because," she continued, "at night, things always seem so much worse than they do in the day, that's why they are called night terrors."

"Is that really all they are?" Daisy asked and her mother replied kindly,

"Yes my love, do you think you alone have them? I can tell you now, you are not the only one. Everybody gets them now and then, young or old and always at night. Can you remember what I used to say to you to help you forget about the worries when you were little?"

"Yes," Daisy replied, "you would say, 'think of something nice, like Christmas morning opening presents, your birthday or when the dog had puppies.'"

"Well there you are, think of happy thoughts."

Daisy thought, then said,

"Well there is this boy at school that makes me laugh..."

"Stop right there, miss," replied Daisy's mother, "now it is me who is going to have night terrors!" Daisy and her mother both laughed.

Daisy felt much better about her father and was soon able to sleep.

The next day Daisy got up and went down stairs, where she was greeted by her mother. "How are you this morning my love?"

"I'm fine now, thank you Mum."

"See I told you everything would seem much better in the morning." said Daisy's mother.

"But how is Dad doing?" Daisy asked,

"Much better, but he is going to have to take it easy for a few days. Anyway you have got to concentrate on your school work, and I've got my eye on you! Boys that make you laugh, indeed!"

Later that very same day just as the sun was setting, Daisy's mother noticed that again there was something bothering her.

That night it was getting late and Daisy called,

"I'm off to bed now."

"Alright my love," said her mother, "I will be up in a minute."

91

Daisy's mother knocked softly on her bedroom door.
"You can come in, I'm all ready for bed."
Daisy's mother went in and sat on the bed saying,
"So what is it then my love? I can see something is bothering you."
"How did you know?"
"Well, let's call it a Mum's intuition! What is worrying you?"
"You know the boy at school that makes me laugh?"
"Yes." replied Daisy's mother.
"Well, he didn't even talk to me today. Do you think he doesn't like me? Have I got an ugly face?" Daisy started to gabble again.
"Stop right there my girl. You are very pretty and you don't have to worry about anything like that yet. You need to study, not be thinking about boy's liking you. You have plenty of time for that later!"
Daisy couldn't hold it in any longer and burst out with laughter.
"I was just teasing you Mum!"
"You cheeky monkey! I think I won't be sleeping tonight, I will be lying awake giggling."

So if ever you can't get to sleep because something is bothering you, just think of nice thoughts, everything just seems so much worse in the night.
Or is it?!

THE MISTLETOE

L ong, long ago when the world was young, there was a small low growing plant called Mistletoe.

Nothing ever noticed it. Mistletoe would just be there, low on the ground, hidden away where nothing could see it and Mistletoe never stopped complaining!

"Oh, I hate what I am. Nothing, nothing ever sees me down here, hidden away amongst the other bushes that have lovely coloured flowers. All I have are white berries that nothing ever looks at! I want to be tall like the trees, not down here in the dirt, I hate the dirt!"

A nearby tree heard Mistletoe complaining.

"What is the matter with you down there?" Asked Tree.

"I don't want to be down here," whined Mistletoe, "I want to be tall like you and not down here in the dirt, I hate the dirt! When it rains, it splashes dirt all over me. When the wind blows, it blows dirt all over my nice glossy green leaves, then they look dirty and dull. I want to be seen and admired. I want things to see me and say 'look at Mistletoe, how fine it looks with its glossy leaves and fine white berries.'" it continued, "Nothing ever sees me down here, hidden away and in the dirt, I hate the dirt!"

The tree was kind, and said,

"Well if only I could see you, I could give you some comfort by bending my branch down and hugging you with my leaves."

Mistletoe thought it would like that.

"Here I am! Down here! If only I was not stuck to these roots in the dirt, I could come out where you could see me!"

"What a good idea," replied Tree, "you could come out and I could pick you up and hold you in my branches, high up here with me. It would be so nice to have the company."

Mistletoe thought that would be wonderful, for everything would then be able to see it up there.

"I wish I could," said Mistletoe.

Tree felt sorry for Mistletoe, the tree was old and had seen many things, like when two branches join and graft themselves together. The tree thought and thought.

"There is a way," said Tree suddenly, "if you can leave your roots, I could pick you up and you could graft yourself onto one of my branches. Then you would not need the roots down there in the dirt and you would be seen by everything! I could give you everything you need that the roots can give you, up here with me where everything can see you."

Mistletoe thought it would like that and said to the tree,

"In the winter when you lose your leaves, mine are still green and I will have white berries. Everything will say, 'look at that fine tree, even in winter there are fine leaves and white berries!'"

"Oh, yes," said Tree, "how fine we would look together, but we must wait until the next rain comes, then you could leave your roots and I will lift you up into my branches."

"Why do I have to wait until the next rain, why can't I do it now?" replied Mistletoe impatiently.

"You have to wait, for if you leave your roots when it is sunny you would dry out too quickly, and grafting yourself to one of my branches will not work."

Days passed and Mistletoe waited very impatiently,

"Oh come on rain, fall from the sky. I have waited days and it's not rained once."

Two weeks passed and every day Mistletoe complained that it had still not rained.

Then one day the clouds started building up, one spot, then another and then a third spot, the rain then fell.
"Is it now the time?" called Mistletoe to Tree.
"Yes, now is the time." replied the tree.

Mistletoe left its roots and the tree bent its branch down and lifted Mistletoe high up into the tree.
"Here," said Tree, "you must graft yourself into my branches."
Mistletoe worked hard, quickly grafting itself into the tree's branches.

Year after year, Mistletoe still didn't stop complaining. For half the year, nothing could see Mistletoe when the tree had its leaves, but when the leaves fell in the autumn, Mistletoe boasted how wonderful it made the tree look and how fine it was, now all things could see it so high in the tree.
Tree soon realised the mistake it had made when it lifted Mistletoe up into its branches, six months of complaining then six months of boasting!

Then the birds came, for now they too could see Mistletoe high up in the branches! They would help themselves to Mistletoe's berries and all day Mistletoe would complain,
"Get off me, leave my berries alone."
The birds took the sticky berries that stuck to their beaks and they wiped them off on other trees, who in turn too started to grow mistletoe in their branches.
The trees had no rest from that time on.
The complaining got worse. People started to arrive and they too saw Mistletoe high up in the trees. The people thought how green

and fine Mistletoe looked,with its white berries, once the tree leaves had all gone.

They too helped themselves to Mistletoe. They also took whole pieces of it, leaves and berries too, to brighten their homes and to steal kisses off one another when it was deep into winter. Mistletoe gave them hope that spring and warmth would return once more.

But that never stopped Mistletoe complaining! How the tree wished it had never lifted Mistletoe up into its branches!

TOMKIN

Tomkin was one of the fairy folk and a rather mischievous pixie at that! He liked nothing better than to make trouble wherever he could. Tomkin would always be on the look-out for any opportunity and human folk were always the perfect target as most human folk could not see him. There was a particular type of mischief he just loved to play on them.....

One fine summer day, Tomkin was walking along the road that went through a little village, when he saw a shop. The door was half open as the day was so lovely and warm.

Tomkin peered around the door and saw that the shop was split into two, with a cobbler one side making and mending shoes and a seamstress on the other making dresses and alterations. The cobbler and seamstress were husband and wife.

"This is going to be lots of fun for me," thought Tomkin, so he slipped quietly through the door.

Tomkin took the pins the seamstress was using to turn up the hem on a dress and hid them. They were still near the seamstress, but out of sight. Next, he took the cobbler's hammer and again hid it just out of his sight.

"Husband," called the seamstress, "have you moved my pins?"

"Why would I move your pins, my dear?" the cobbler replied.

"Well, I had them just here a moment ago and now they are gone!"

"They can't be far, my love!" said the cobbler.

The seamstress stood up and looked all about her work space,
"Ah, there they are. That's so strange, I don't remember putting them there."
A few minutes later, the cobbler called out,
"Wife, have you moved my hammer?"
"Now why would I move your hammer?" replied the seamstress, "I have been over here all the time my dear and haven't been near your workbench."
"Well, I swear I had it one minute and the next it was gone!"
He then stood up and looked around his work bench.
"Don't worry my dear, I've found it. Now that is strange, I don't remember putting it there."
Tomkin was taking such a delight in his tricks, that he started to sing a funny little song to himself,

"Tomkin hides your hammer and pins,
It brings the smile that Tomkin grins."

Tomkin went over to the seamstress, who was back to pinning her hem and took her scissors and popped them in her apron pocket. He then went over to the cobbler, removed a piece of cut leather off his work bench and put it underneath.
Tomkin sat on a chair and waited for the chaos to unravel.
The cobbler was getting just a little frustrated by now.
"Where on earth has that piece of leather gone?" he said, placing his hands on his hips, "I have only just cut it out. I put it here and now it's gone!"
The seamstress tutted and looked over,
"Is that it, right there under your bench?"
The cobbler looked and said,
"Well bless my soul, however did it get down there?"
"You must have knocked it off, you clumsy oaf!"
"How very strange," replied the cobbler, looking most confused, "I don't remember knocking it off?"
"How would you remember knocking it off?" laughed the seamstress and then teased her husband saying,

"Oh, I think I shall just knock this piece of leather off the bench and onto the floor!"

"Stop mocking me woman," said the cobbler crossly.

"Ha, ha," laughed the seamstress, "you will get over it my dear." then rolled an off cut piece of fabric and threw it at her husband. It hit him right between the eyes.

"Hey, you could have had my eye out with that!"

The seamstress laughed again saying,

"What with a soft piece of cloth?"

Tomkin was loving this.

Then came a shout from the seamstress,

"For goodness sake, where are my scissors now? Have you used them, Husband, to cut out that piece of leather?"

"No, I used a knife and anyway, I have my own scissors, you daft woman!"

The seamstress lent forward to look for the scissors and felt a slight stab in her leg. Feeling around to see what had caused it, she found the scissors in her apron pocket. "Oh, here they are. I think I must be losing my mind, I never put my scissors in my apron pocket!"

Tomkin, being very pleased with his work, started to sing once more.

"Tomkin hides your hammer and pins,
It brings the smile that Tomkin grins.
Tomkin hides your scissors and leather,
The fun I have is getting better and better."

"Husband," asked the seamstress a few minutes later, "can you help me? I have these two seams held together, could you pass me a needle and thread please, so I can tack them?"

Quick as a flash Tomkin took the needle and thread then stuck it into the cuff of the seamstresses sleeve.

"Where is it my dear?" asked the cobbler.

"It's in the pin cushion."

The cobbler looked,

"No it's not," he said.

"You're not looking! It's just there, the needle with the white thread." replied the seamstress pointing to her pincushion.

" Er, no it's not here."

"Ahh, it is. I have just put it there!" said the seamstress. She let go of the seams she was holding, to show her husband where it was, muttering under her breath,

"Why do I bother? If you want something doing, you have to do it yourself. It's right there!" The seamstress reached out her hand and pointed to where she had put the needle and thread just a moment ago.

"Oh, it's not there!"

The cobbler looked to where his wife was pointing.

"There it is! It's stuck in your sleeve, you crazy woman. You're taking me away from my work, when you had it all the time!"

"Well how very strange, I didn't put it there, I'm sure of it."

"Well who do you think did?" the cobbler teased, "Do you think there is someone else doing it? Come on out you sneaky thief!"

"No," replied his wife, "it's just me, I must be going completely mad!"

"You and me both, I think." sighed the cobbler.

Tomkin was now laughing to himself so hard that he almost fell off the chair he was sitting on.

"It's time for me to leave." he whispered and jumped out of his chair and started to sing to himself once more as he slipped out the door.

"Tomkin hides your hammer and pins,
It brings the smile that Tomkin grins,
Tomkin hides your scissors and leather,
The fun I have it's getting better and better,
Tomkin hides your needle and thread,
You think you're going mad in the head!"

Tomkin may have visited the cobbler and seamstress again, but who knows if he did have even more of his favourite mischief with them and if they ever discovered the truth!

But just know this, when you are busy and you put something down and can't find it again, but then it turns up in some random place, you might think to yourself, "How did it get there?"
Perhaps Tomkin has paid you a visit!

A YOUNG LADS WIT

L ong ago, there was a man named Will, who worked very hard on the land. Every day he would get up, help feed his family, then off he went, out to work in the fields or in the orchard, come rain or shine. The toil was hard, but Will was always happy in his work.

His family were young, far too young to help with any of his work out in the fields.

One day he decided that he would have to take on one of his neighbours' lads to help him in the fields.

Now this lad was cocky and thought himself to be the best thing ever.

The lad came round to the house to see Will about working for him. Will asked the lad, "Are you strong enough to work all day when the sun is hot and when the winter is so cold that you feel it bite at your fingers and toes?"

"Of course I am," boasted the lad, very sure of himself, "nothing will get the better of me!"

"Are you sure of that?" Will said.

"Oh yes," replied the lad, "I can keep up with anyone, you don't need to worry about me!"

"I think I already am!" Will said wryly.

"No no, I will be here ready to start long before you are each morning, just you see if I'm not!"

Will just grinned slightly, a quirky smile, one side more than the other. The lad had no idea what he was up against, for one thing Will loved was a challenge and Will was no fool!

"Alright," said Will, "You can start at 8 o'clock sharp, tomorrow morning."

"8 o'clock? I can start earlier than that. Why, it would be good for me!" replied the lad. Will just shook his head and said,

"You haven't seen 7 o'clock recently have you? It's late autumn and it's still dark at that time and I wouldn't want you stumbling around in the dark, treading on everything. 8 o'clock it is!"

"Alright." the lad agreed.

"I will see you in the morning and we will see how you get on, oh and you might want to wrap up warm." replied Will smiling.

The first morning the lad turned up early like he had said.

"See, I'm here before you old man!"

"We will see if the same is said for tomorrow." replied Will. Will and the lad worked hard all day, digging over the soil, but Will had dug two rows to each of the lad's one.

"I thought you said you could keep up with anyone?" Will said with a chuckle in his voice.

"I am trying." said the lad.

"You definitely are that!" laughed Will.

"Don't worry I'm just teasing you. You will get up to speed soon enough. It's all about the technique and the swing of it. All will come in good time, I can't help it if you are lazy!" Will was still chuckling to himself.

On the second day the lad was a little later getting to Will. It was still before 8 o'clock, but the lad was so stiff and aching from all the hard work the day before.

The weather was turning a bit colder with clear skies and an East-erly wind.

"I see you're getting lazier, as I was here before you today!" Will teased. The lad couldn't think of anything smart to reply.

"I hope you have wrapped up warm, you don't want the weather to get the better of you, do you?"

"Well I was hot enough yesterday!" replied the lad defiantly.

"We are going out to the orchard today, there will not be so much moving about. I don't want you getting cold." said Will.

"Oh, I won't get cold, not me." answer the lad, his bravado returning.

After a few hours out in the orchard, Will noticed the lad getting slower and slower. He called to the lad with a cheeky grin,

"Are you alright, or are you just being lazy over there?" The lad turned to answer, but when Will saw the lad's face, he noticed his lips looked blue.

"Right, I'm getting you into the warm." and he took the lad back to his own house.

Will got the lad in by the stove, inside his cottage and gave him some warm soup. When Will saw the colour starting to return to the lad's face and his lips no longer blue, he teased him a little,

"Well I can't believe you will go to any lengths to get out of work!"

"I didn't mean to stop, I can go back out there now." mumbled the lad.

"It's alright," said Will "you best stop here a little while longer."

On the third day the lad was a minute late.

"Well lazy bones, you're late."

"Sorry, It's just every part of me hurts," moaned the lad.

"I thought you were going to be here before me each morning, that you could keep up with anyone and nothing would get the better of you? This sort of work takes time to get used to and you have to build up to it, but for now I think you are just being lazy!" Will was teasing him and had that quirky grin that was slightly on one side more than the other.

"I'm not lazy, I'm not!" cried the lad.

"I'm just getting the better of you." explained Will.

"No you won't!" answered the lad.

"Oh dear lord above!" exclaimed Will, "you must be lazy then."

"No I'm not." replied the lad sulkily.

"Alright I will prove it to you then. I bet that you wouldn't even go a mile before giving up."

"I wouldn't give up, not I." said the lad.

"Ahh, I bet you would even if you had a day to do it." said Will.

"I could easily go a mile no problem." said the lad.

"No, I think you are far too lazy," Will was trying hard to contain his laughter.

"Well I bet you I could." said the lad, he was starting to get very annoyed.

"Alright," replied Will, "I will give you the direction and you have to travel a mile. For instance, if I said North you would have to travel one mile North, it doesn't have to be in a straight line as long as it's North, Yes?"

"Yes, of course," said the lad, "I bet this week's wages on it that I can."

"Alright," agreed Will and held out his hand to shake on the bet. Will could hardly speak for chuckling by now.

"Right, you have one day from now to travel one mile and to make it easier for you I will give you two directions to choose from. You can decide which way to go."

"Hold it," said the lad, thinking how easily he was going to win the bet "so if I had a horse could I use that?"

"You, my dear boy can use whatever you like." Will replied holding back the tears of laughter.

"Let's have it then, which two ways is it?"

Will looked at the lad with that quirky smile of his and said,

"Up or down!"

The lad just looked dumbfounded and speechless, for quite a while and then said

"I think perhaps I still have a lot to learn!"

"Yes," answered Will, " but don't worry, I will still give you your weeks wages, because I think from now on we will get along just fine!"

THE LITTLE
WOODEN BOX

T here once was a husband and wife who had two very young children and they all lived in a small house on the edge of town.

The husband needed to get his wife an anniversary gift, for in two days' time they would have been married for five years.

"Now," the husband thought to himself, "five wonderful years it will be this year, I wonder what would be a fine gift for a five-year anniversary?"
The husband had always wanted to give his wife an eternity ring, but he could never afford one, especially one with diamonds or even perhaps just one diamond. The family never seemed to have any spare money for such luxury things like an expensive eternity ring.

The husband decided that he was going to go into town to see what he could find. He walked down the main street, past most of the shops he would normally visit in the town, trying to get some inspiration of what he may buy his wife for their anniversary.

As he walked further down the street, he noticed a little, slightly dim looking alleyway. At the end of the alleyway he could see a funny little shop with dark red cracked paint that had just started to flake off in a few places. Above the shop hung a little sign that had gold lettering on it, saying 'Antiquities and things'.

The husband was intrigued by this shop as he had not noticed it before. Not that he would have done, for when he usually went into town, he knew what he needed and in which shops to find it. He had not aimlessly wandered around the town before in search of something that he wasn't quite sure of what to buy.

The husband went to the shop door and gently pushed it open. A little bell rang as it hit the door. An old man appeared, with a neat white beard and spectacles perched on the end of his nose, his eyes peering over the top of the spectacles.

"Can I help you," enquired the shopkeeper.

"Do you mind if I look around, I'm looking for an anniversary gift for my wife?"

"Not at all," said the shopkeeper, "and if you don't mind my asking, which anniversary will it be?"

"It's our fifth, but I'm not sure what I should give my wife for a fifth anniversary?"

The shopkeeper smiled and replied,

"It is a wooden gift that you should give for a fifth anniversary." The husband thanked the shopkeeper and looked around the shop.

There were all sorts of interesting and strange items for sale in the little shop. The husband saw a few glass domed shaped jars with wooden bases and some strange things inside that he didn't like to ask what they were! There were small bits of unusual and quirky furniture, all sorts of different boxes, some with things in, some without and some little bottles that had corks in with differ-ent colored ribbons tied around the top. There was a glass cabinet with jewelry in that caught the husband's eye.

The husband went over to have a look at the beautiful things in-side the glass cabinet. As he was taking everything in, he noticed on the bottom shelf of the cabinet a tiny silver ring. It had caught his attention, for it was so bright and shiny. He opened the cabinet and had a closer look, it was beautiful with just a very subtle delicate pattern running around it. He looked at the price tag. It was a good price and he could perhaps get something else to go with it. The husband carried on looking when he saw, in amongst some bits piled on a small table that there was a small wooden box. The box had been beautifully carved with flowers and a little brass plate set into the wood with a pattern on it. The pattern looked like a single line running down the middle, with lines going across. Some lines were straight, some at a slight angle and some with more lines than the others. Some of the smaller lines were on one side of the line down the middle, some on the other and one that looked like a little flag sticking out from the line.

The husband took the box to the shopkeeper and asked, "There is a very unusual pattern on the brass plate on this box, do you know what it is?" The shopkeeper looked at the box and said, "Oh of course, it looks like ogam, an ancient type of writing. I have no idea what it means, but ogam spelt backwards says 'mago', which means wizard in Spanish, though I'm sure that that is only coincidental."
"I would like to buy this box and the ring please," said the husband. "That's a fine choice." replied the shopkeeper, handing over the two gifts. The husband placed the ring in the box for safekeeping on the journey home.

The day of the anniversary came and the husband gave the box to his wife saying, "Here I have something wooden for you for our fifth anniversary," then he kissed his wife and said,

"Open it, there is something else for you inside."

The husband looked so pleased as his wife slowly opened the box, then she looked at her husband and smiling back at him, she said, "I love the box, but there is nothing inside it!"

"What?" exclaimed the husband, then he looked in the box and cried,

"Oh no, it must have fallen out when I was carrying it home. I wanted to get you an eternity ring but could not afford it, but instead I found a beautiful silver ring. Oh what do I do? I wish I'd never bought the box and put the ring inside it."

Just as the husband finished saying those words the box vanished. The husband and the wife were totally dumbfounded by the box's disappearance. When the husband had gathered his senses he said,

"I'm going back to the shop. I want some answers!"

The husband marched back to the little shop of 'Antiquities and things', pushed the door open and rang the little bell again. As he entered, the shopkeeper said,

"Ah, you have come to collect the box and ring. I put it to one side for you just in case you did want it after all."

The husband was so taken aback he could not think of what to say, then muttered,

"I will just check to see if I have enough money to buy it."

When the husband opened his wallet, he found that he had the same money in there as before he had bought the box and ring the first time! Not wanting to let on to the shopkeeper that there was something quite strange about the box, the husband paid again and left the shop and made his way home. Only this time he did not put the ring in the box!

When the husband got home, he called out to his wife,

"You are not going to believe this." then produced the box and the ring.

"Oh the ring is really beautiful, thank you so much," she said with such delight and the husband explained all that had happened.

They took the box and set it on the table and placed a nut in it, shut the lid, then opened it again, but the nut was still there!

"What is it about the ring that made it disappear?"

"It is a silver ring, yes?" said the wife, "well, what have we got that is silver but small, that will fit in the box?" The husband replied,

"It will have to be small as we don't have anything silver that is big, or come to think of it not much that is small either!"

"Ah, but what about a broken piece of necklace that is silver?" asked the wife, then she went and found her jewelry box that had an old broken silver necklace in it. She took out the necklace and placed it inside the little wooden box.

"I hope you don't want that anymore," said the husband, "because I don't think we're going to be getting it back if it does disappear at all!"

"But you wished you had not bought the box and stored the ring safely inside it and they both went back to the shop, as if you had not bought them at all! Hopefully we could wish again and there is only one way to find out."

The husband closed the lid of the box and said,

"Right, we had better think of a good wish or that silver necklace might be wasted."

The husband and the wife thought for a while and then the wife said,

"How about wealth to come our way?"

"Oh that is good, I like that," the husband replied.

He then opened the box and the silver necklace had gone.

"I do wish wealth would come our way then." he said with a wry smile.

From that day on, the husband and wife were never in want for anything ever again.

If you should be walking down the street and there is a little side alley with a funny little shop with dark red, cracked flaking paint and a little sign above it with gold writing on that says 'Antiquities and things', it might be worth having a look inside! There may be something worth buying in that shop, because it means that shop is still there.

ACKNOWLEDGEMENT

Trisha Kelland for book cover design and illustrations
To my family for the inspiration

Printed in Poland
by Amazon Fulfillment
Poland Sp. z o.o., Wrocław
04 October 2021

25c4ba7c-b860-4b59-8d6d-938b454383c7R01